THE FORTUNES OF TEXAS

Follow the lives and loves of a wealthy family with a rich history and deep ties in the Lone Star State

THE HOTEL FORTUNE

Check in to the Hotel Fortune, the Fortune brothers' latest venture in cozy Rambling Rose, Texas. They're scheduled to open on Valentine's Day, when a suspicious accident damages a balcony—and injures one of the workers! Now the future of the hotel could be in jeopardy. *Was* the crash an accident— or is something more nefarious going on?

Wiley Fortune is a big-city attorney who doesn't like to lose—in the courtroom or in life. So far, he's found little to like about the sleepy Texas town most of his family has made their home...until Grace Williams falls (literally!) into his arms. But Wiley's visit is supposed to be temporary—and he knows better than to date a family employee! The last thing he needs is a relationship that makes him want more...

Dear Reader,

Happy 2021! I hope this is a wonderful year for you, and I'm thrilled to kick it off with the first book in the latest Fortunes of Texas series.

My favorite heroines are the ones who aren't actually looking for romance but instead want to find their place in the world—and they find a love that helps them get there. Grace Williams has returned to her hometown of Rambling Rose after a few hard knocks. But she's determined to make a new start at the Hotel Fortune. And when she—quite literally—falls for Wiley Fortune, Grace discovers the perfect man for her.

Big-city attorney Wiley Fortune can appreciate that his siblings are happy in the small Texas town, but he doesn't plan to stay. Wiley values his independence and has worked hard for his career. But when Grace is injured minutes after their first fateful meeting, Wiley learns that when you fall for the right person, fighting to make a love that lasts is more important than anything else.

I hope you enjoy reading Wiley and Grace's story as much as I loved writing it.

Please come say hi on Facebook or at michellemajor.com.

Happy reading!

Michelle

Her Texas New Year's Wish

———

MICHELLE MAJOR

HARLEQUIN
SPECIAL
EDITION

Special thanks and acknowledgment are given to Michelle Major for her contribution to the The Fortunes of Texas: The Hotel Fortune miniseries.

HARLEQUIN®

SPECIAL EDITION™

Recycling programs for this product may not exist in your area.

ISBN-13: 978-1-335-40458-9

Her Texas New Year's Wish

Harlequin Enterprises ULC
22 Adelaide St. West, 40th Floor
Toronto, Ontario M5H 4E3, Canada
www.Harlequin.com

Printed in U.S.A.

Michelle Major grew up in Ohio but dreamed of living in the mountains. Soon after graduating with a degree in journalism, she pointed her car west and settled in Colorado. Her life and house are filled with one great husband, two beautiful kids, a few furry pets and several well-behaved reptiles. She's grateful to have found her passion writing stories with happy endings. Michelle loves to hear from her readers at michellemajor.com.

To the Fortunes of Texas team—
thanks for making this journey so much fun.

Chapter One

"I wouldn't drink that if I were you."

Wiley Fortune plucked the glass from his sister's hand and placed it back on the polished mahogany bar.

Nicole gave him a funny look. "It's water, Wi. Roja is providing the food for this party. I may be a guest, but I'm also still on the clock."

"I know it's water." Wiley tugged on the end of Nicole's long blond hair, the way he used to do when they were kids. "That's my point."

Nicole, Ashley and Megan Fortune—the triplets— had been born seven years after Wiley, miracle babies in every sense of the word. Their parents, David and Marci, had married after a whirlwind courtship, blending four sons from their respective first marriages in a way that would have made Carol Brady's head spin back in the day.

The boys had gotten off to a bit of a rocky start as they attempted to figure out their roles in the new family. Everything had changed when his mom gave birth to Stephanie five years later. One thing all four boys could agree on was how much they adored their baby sister. Mom had hoped to add another sibling to the mix right away, but she'd had trouble conceiving. Although she'd tried to hide her emotional pain and physical exhaustion, Wiley knew that season of loss had taken a toll on her.

Wiley loved every member of his family, but he'd been a quiet, introverted kid and it was a lot to grow up in such a big, boisterous family. Maybe that fact had something to do with the distance that had seemed to grow between him and the rest of his siblings.

He was the only one who hadn't migrated to the quaint town of Rambling Rose, Texas, although they'd convinced him to visit over Christmas and return for his cousin Adam Fortune's son's first birthday party.

"What's wrong with the water in Rambling Rose?" Nicole asked, scrunching her perfect nose.

"It's obviously tainted," Wiley said, keeping his features neutral and using the same tone with her that he did for contract negotiations in his law firm back in Chicago. "Look around at all the nauseatingly happy couples here tonight. Something happens when a Fortune drinks the Rambling Rose water. They lose all sense and succumb to Cupid's arrow."

Nicole rolled her bright blue eyes toward the tile ceiling that had just been installed in the restaurant. "I guess that explains why you're on your second whiskey of the night."

He lifted the etched-glass tumbler in her direction. "Much safer. Can I buy you a drink?"

"I'm running the restaurant and bar tonight," Nicole said with a delicate sniff. "I don't need you to buy me a drink."

She swatted his arm, then grabbed the water and made a show of drinking down half of it in a few gulps. "Besides—" she delicately dabbed at the corner of her mouth with the flowing sleeve of her batik-print dress "—what's wrong with love?"

"It's a distraction," he answered without hesitation.

"That's cynical, Wiley, even for you." Nicole climbed onto the bar stool next to him and swiveled so that they were both facing out toward the crowd. "Look at how happy Callum and Dillon are."

She pointed toward their brothers, who stood near the front of the banquet room greeting guests. Dillon stood close to Hailey Miller, his fiancée, whom he'd met because she worked at the local spa the family had opened in town last year, while Callum and his wife, Becky, held hands. They'd met and quickly married after Callum moved to Rambling Rose and fell in love with the sweet nurse and her adorable twin toddlers, Sasha and Luna.

"It's the water," he repeated. "Or they've all been stricken by the Texas heat. Even Steven is all googly-eyed for his lady. I barely recognize my own brothers."

A second sister, Megan, let out a mild laugh as she approached from the other side of him and helped herself to a sip of his drink. "If you don't recognize your brothers, it's because you spend too much time on your own."

"I'm here now," Wiley muttered.

"Because Mom guilted you into it," Megan reminded him. She, Nicole and Ashley looked almost identical with their shiny hair and delicate features. They'd followed their brothers to Rambling Rose and opened a farm-to-table restaurant, Provisions, to a great deal of success. Megan was the most serious of the trio and handled the finances for both Provisions and Roja, located inside the Hotel Fortune, which was due to open in just over a month. Nicole was the more flamboyantly creative and was using her culinary skills to create an innovative menu for Roja as the restaurant's executive chef. Ashley took on the role of bossy micromanager in the best way possible, and as the general manager for Provisions.

"Wiley thinks Rambling Rose is a bad influence on all of us because the Fortunes are falling in love here."

"You could use some more love in your life."

Megan poked a finger into his biceps. "You work too much."

"How would you know? I live in Chicago. Don't tell me you're keeping tabs on my life from halfway across the country." Wiley felt heat prick the back of his neck as his sisters exchanged a knowing glance. He didn't think he'd sounded defensive, but this was the reason he skipped so many family gatherings. There was no privacy to be had once his brothers and sisters got involved.

"All you talk about is work," Megan answered, smoothing a hand over her cream-colored sweater.

"I like my job." Wiley took a long drink of whiskey, welcoming the burn of the liquor in his throat. "It's fascinating."

"Contract law isn't fascinating." Nicole laughed. "The restaurant business is fascinating. It's always evolving."

"Not to mention there's no shortage of yummy food to taste," Megan added.

"Being an attorney is fascinating to me," Wiley grumbled.

"Because you need more excitement in your life." Nicole turned to him. "Don't you long for a change, Wi? For years, you've been at the same firm in the same position—"

"And living in the same condo." Megan fist-bumped her sister.

"I'm stable and consistent," Wiley told them.

"Boring," Nicole countered.

"When was the last time you did something spontaneous?" Megan demanded, placing a hand on his knee and pinching like she used to when they were kids.

"What the hell?" Wiley squirmed and then shooed away her hand.

"You're still girl-crazy," Megan told him with a laugh. "You always have been."

"You just need to improve your taste," Nicole advised.

Megan nodded. "Maybe then it will last beyond a couple of months."

Wiley resisted the urge to growl or to stomp away the way he had when his baby sisters bothered him when they were younger. He pointed to their cousin, Kane, who'd joined Callum's construction company last year once Callum moved the operation to Rambling Rose. "Go bother Kane with your meddling," he said.

Nicole laughed. "What are we, the Scooby-Doo gang?"

"Those meddling sisters," Megan said, making her voice low like a cartoon villain's.

"You have so many choices of Fortunes to annoy here tonight."

"But you're our current favorite." Megan leaned in and placed a smacking kiss on Wiley's cheek.

"The rest of them aren't half as much fun now that they've found love," Nicole admitted, resting her head on his shoulder as her tone turned wistful. "They're all so blissed out from true love."

"You're still an easy target." Megan smiled at him, but it didn't quite reach her blue eyes.

"Why doesn't that sound like a compliment?"

"We want you to be happy," Megan told him, but Wiley wasn't sure if she was truly talking about him or thinking of herself. He wasn't about to point out that neither Nicole nor Megan had found love in Rambling Rose.

Nicole handed him her nearly empty glass of water. "You should have some of this. If there really is something in the water, it will be good for you."

"You know that was a joke." He took the water from her and finished it in one swallow. "First, I don't believe in true love. It isn't pragmatic, and the odds of it being successful are ridiculously bad. Besides, whatever my future holds, I'm pretty sure it doesn't include finding my perfect match in a town that's no more than a tiny speck on the Texas map. I'm here temporarily to support all of you. Nothing more."

"You have to keep your heart open," Megan told him. "You never know when love will find you." She gestured toward Callum, who lifted one of the twins into the air. "When Callum and Becky met, he wasn't looking for love."

"Now he'd tell you he couldn't imagine his life without Becky, Sasha and Luna."

Wiley sighed. His sisters were right about Callum.

It still felt strange that his brother had taken on the role of father figure to the pretty widow's daughters so seamlessly. Not that Callum wasn't great with kids. He'd had plenty of experience with Stephanie and the triplets. But up until he'd met Becky, Wiley had been certain Callum didn't want kids. The same went for Dillon and Steven. In fact, it had been the change in each of his brothers that made him feel like even more of an odd man out in his family.

He glanced between Nicole and Megan, at the similar wistful expressions as they surveyed the crowd. No way would he rain on their romantic parade, even if he knew their unwavering belief in true love might have more to do with youth and inexperience than anything else. Wiley had been around the dating block enough to know that some people weren't cut out for love. People like him.

His siblings had a lot to be proud of. They'd accomplished so much in their time in Rambling Rose. He'd watched from a distance with fascination over the past year and half as they'd transformed the sleepy community into a thriving small town.

Wiley smiled as Ashley, the third triplet, approached, wagging her finger. "You three need to mingle."

Ashley had always been the bossiest. Now that she was settled in Rambling Rose and happy with her fiancé, Rodrigo Mendoza, and the success of Provisions, she was even more confident in her ability to order her siblings around.

"We're doing important work here," Megan told Ashley with an arched brow. "Convincing Wiley to move to Rambling Rose."

"He's about to agree." Nicole nodded.

"That's wonderful." Ashley gave Wiley a tight hug.

"And a total lie." He extricated himself from her embrace and held up his empty glass toward the bartender, silently requesting a refill. He was staying out at the Fame and Fortune Ranch where several of his siblings lived, so Nicole had given him a ride to the hotel tonight. Might as well take advantage, especially with his sisters on a mission.

"Larkin is a cute baby," he said casually, then smiled to himself as the triplets began to talk over one another, extolling the virtues of the birthday boy.

Nothing distracted them like an adorable kid.

He thanked the bartender when the man brought him a fresh glass and took a step away from the triplets. Time to make a quick exit from that conversation.

Steven waved to him, and Wiley started in that direction, then paused when a flash of blue caught his attention. A beautiful woman wearing a tailored cerulean sheath dress.

The party was being held on the second floor of Roja, the signature restaurant that was part of the Hotel Fortune. The boutique hotel, with its Spanish architecture and Western decor that was a nod to the town's history, was the crowning achievement for his brothers. Callum, Dillon and Steven had successfully opened various businesses in town over the past year, from the medical clinic to a spa to several upscale retail shops. He knew they'd received the most push-back from the community about the initial plan for the hotel, and it had been Kane who'd smoothed over the waters in town, convincing Callum to rescale the project to be smaller and more intimate.

The Hotel Fortune was set to open in just over a month, and Wiley had no doubt it would be a huge success. His brothers and sisters wouldn't settle for anything less.

There were at least fifty people in attendance for Larkin's birthday. In addition to his parents, Adam and Laurel, and his immediate and extended family, the private banquet room on the restaurant's second floor was filled with friends and hotel employees. The community had banded together last year to support the baby when he needed a bone marrow transplant. Everyone was thrilled to celebrate the little boy who'd overcome so much. And to Wiley's surprise, based on how his siblings had talked about the celebration, all the different Fortune factions seemed to be getting along.

He turned toward the wall of windows and patio doors that had been opened for the evening. It was unseasonably warm for this time of year, even by Texas standards. In the center of the exterior wall was a stamped concrete balcony with wrought iron railings that overlooked the patio and pool below.

His gaze snagged on the same woman who'd caught his attention a few moments earlier. She had long, bourbon-colored hair, a slender build and creamy skin from what he could see of her arms in the sleeveless dress she wore. She spoke to Callum and Mariana, one of the town's most illustrious residents, who was working with Nicole as the sous chef in the Roja kitchen. For years, Mariana had run a successful outdoor market in downtown Rambling Rose, with vendors selling all kinds of food and wares. And her food stall had been one of the most—if not the most—popular stand of all. It was in no small part thanks to her influence with the local vendors that the Fortune family had been able to go ahead with some of their most successful new projects, all because Mariana understood that they would bring new life to her hometown.

Wiley didn't recognize the woman in blue, although he couldn't help but think they'd met before. There was nothing else that would explain the strange connection when he hadn't even fully seen her face.

Then she turned, and the breath whooshed out of him on a long exhale. It was like a piece of a puzzle snapping together with its perfect match. His heart seemed to skip a beat. No, that couldn't be right. The woman was a stranger. There was no question, because he would never forget his reaction to her.

She might be a stranger, but he had to meet her.

He made his way through the crowd. Mariana walked away, but Callum remained in conversation with the woman as Wiley stopped just behind his brother.

"Hey, Wi." Callum glanced over his shoulder. "Have you met Grace Williams? She's one of our management trainees. Grace, this is my brother Wiley. He's our big-shot family attorney visiting from Chicago."

Wiley barely registered the introduction as Grace smiled at him. Her eyes, the same bright blue of a clear summer sky, crinkled at the corners.

"Hi." He struggled to regain control over the rapid cadence of his breathing. If he didn't know better, Wiley would think he was having some sort of heart attack. There was no logical explanation for his re-action. He'd met countless beautiful women over the years and dated his fair share of them. But Grace Williams leveled him with just a smile.

Callum cleared his throat, and Wiley realized Grace had offered her hand to shake.

"It's nice to meet you," she said softly, a blush staining her cheeks.

He took her hand, almost expecting to feel the zap of an electric current when he touched her. No literal shock, which he realized was a ridiculous expecta-tion in the first place.

"Hey, Wiley," Steven called from a few feet away. "Come over here for a second. I have a couple hotel employees I want you to meet."

Wiley had already met a dozen new people tonight, employees, local business owners and members of the extended Fortune family. He'd enjoyed the various introductions until this moment. Now he was done talking to people other than Grace.

"It's fine," Callum told him with a dismissive pat on the shoulder. "Grace and I are discussing some hotel business, anyway."

Wiley wanted to argue, but that would be rude. He looked toward Grace once more and her breath hitched.

"I'll be around all night," she told him, darting a quick glance toward Callum before her gaze returned to Wiley. "I hope we can chat some more."

"Definitely," he told her, the band around his heart loosening slightly. He had all night to talk to Grace.

That thought calmed Wiley enough so that he could shift his attention to Steven as he walked away. He wasn't about to lose his chance with Grace when they'd only just met.

Wiley Fortune was quite possibly the most handsome man Grace had ever seen. And in his family, that was saying something.

He shared the same tall, lean build as Steven and that innate Fortune spark, but Grace's reaction to Wiley had been unexpected. As he walked away, she worked to regain control. The last thing she needed was to make a spectacle of herself in front of Callum.

She did her best not to fidget as she gave an update on the water heater that had leaked in one of the hotel's main-floor utility rooms. She hated relaying anything that seemed like bad news, especially in the middle of a first birthday party, but hoped the fact that she had a solution for the potential dilemma would help.

"It sounds like you handled it perfectly," Callum told her, and she let out a small sigh of relief. "Just like tonight. Larkin's celebration has gone off without a hitch."

"I can't take all the credit," Grace admitted because that was her way. "The Roja staff has done an amazing job. Everyone's pitched in where they were supposed to. And a roomful of Fortunes isn't as intimidating as you led me to believe."

Callum grinned. "We're on our best behavior." He leaned closer. "It's a bit of a surprise, I'll admit. This night makes me feel like we're actually on track for the grand opening next month."

"Definitely," Grace agreed. "By then, all the details will be ironed out. Everyone in Rambling Rose is going to be talking about the Hotel Fortune."

"I hope you're right. This venture has definitely given us the most headaches, although it will all be worth it when we have a full slate of guests."

"You and your brothers and sisters have made sure every step of the redevelopment plan for the town has been thoughtfully crafted and executed. I'm honored to be a part of it." Grace inwardly cringed, hoping she didn't sound like a total suck-up, but Callum smiled.

"We're glad to have you on the team. I'm sorry things at Cowboy Country didn't work out, but their loss is our gain."

Grace forced a smile, although mention of her previous job had her stomach tightening painfully. She didn't think anyone in Rambling Rose knew the full truth of why she'd left the cowboy theme park run by another branch of the Fortune family in the town of Horseback Hollow. There was no way she was going to share her heartbreak and humiliation, not when her life was finally getting back on track.

"Take a break." Callum gestured to the row of food tables. "Have a piece of cake or a drink or just enjoy the beautiful night. You've earned it, Grace."

She nodded. "Thanks. I'll have a piece of birthday cake. I'm glad things are going so well and Larkin's enjoying the attention."

Someone called to Callum, and she turned for the cake table but first detoured toward the empty balcony overlooking the hotel's impeccably landscaped pool area. She needed to cool off as she could still feel her cheeks burning from the way Wiley had looked at her.

She wouldn't jeopardize her future for any man, no matter how attractive. In some ways, she still felt like pinching herself, because despite all the things that had gone wrong in her life, the three and half months she'd spent in the Hotel Fortune management training program seemed to make all the trouble worth it.

Yes, she'd had to drop out of college to help take care of her older brother after he'd been seriously injured in a car accident almost a decade earlier. Yes, she'd struggled to fit in when she'd finally returned to school, unable to enjoy life in the way regular college students did. She'd been too serious and too focused, determined to get her degree but always guilty that she was able to have a life Jake couldn't due to his recovery. After finally graduating with a degree in hospitality management, she'd landed a job in the Cowboy Country front office. At that point, Grace thought she was finally on her way. She'd had a good job, a handsome boyfriend and a fresh start in life.

Discovering that Craig had been cheating on her with a fellow employee—and that pretty much everyone at Cowboy Country knew it except Grace—had been a blow she hadn't expected. One that brought her to her knees, literally and figuratively.

But she was leaving the past behind for her new future with the Hotel Fortune. Although members of the family had been taking the lead on running things during construction, they planned to promote someone from within the training program to the role of general manager as part of the grand opening. There might be other employees vying for the coveted position, but Grace was determined to earn it.

She stepped to the edge of the balcony, running her palms across the smooth wrought iron railing. She couldn't remember ever feeling such a sense of anticipation as she did at this moment.

Drawing in a long pull of the fresh air from the open patio doors, she turned back toward the party. Pride swelled in her chest at the crowd of happy people. She'd had a lot to do with making this evening a success.

Her gaze snagged on Wiley once again as he moved away from the group where he stood. One corner of his full mouth tugged into a sexy smirk, like he could feel the way her body went on high alert from across the room. Grace felt like she was on a roller coaster, climbing the track of the first giant hill. Her heart raced as she thought about the free fall to come.

When he started toward her, she turned and leaned forward, gripping the railing with rigid fingers. It wasn't that she didn't want to meet him. In fact, her body practically yearned to get close to him.

But she'd given herself to a man once before with disastrous results. No way would she fall again.

A loud crack split the air, and she stumbled as the balcony pitched forward. Then she was falling so fast she didn't even have time to scream.

Chapter Two

"This doesn't make any sense." Callum dashed a hand through his hair as he paced the small waiting room in the Rambling Rose Medical Center emergency room. "In all my years of construction, I've never had something like that happen on one of our projects."

"We'll figure out what caused it," Wiley said from where he sat on a patterned chair situated against the far wall. "But first we need to make sure Grace is okay. She's the priority right now."

Callum nodded. "You're right. But what if it had been a hotel guest or one of the kids on that balcony when it collapsed? Can you imagine if there were people on the patio below?"

Wiley understood his brother's train of thought but felt oddly defensive at the subtle suggestion that the accident wasn't as catastrophic because a mere employee had been injured.

As if sensing his irritation, Callum held up a hand. He wore dark slacks and a button-down shirt that was covered with dust from the rubble of the mess that had been made when the balcony collapsed. "I'm not insinuating that Grace is disposable. I would never put her or any employee at risk. You know that, Wi."

"She was unconscious," Wiley muttered, his nerve endings pulling tight at the memory of the EMTs lifting her limp body onto a stretcher. "She could have died in that fall."

The thought of losing her before he got to know her felt like a punch to the gut.

"But she woke up in the ambulance." Callum continued to pace back and forth. "She was obviously in shock but seemed lucid. Her ankle was in bad shape, but I have to believe that's the worst of her injuries. We need to believe Grace will be okay."

Grace Williams.

Callum had shared the woman's name with the first responders when they arrived at the hotel mere minutes after Nicole made the 911 call.

In the chaos that ensued after the balcony's collapse, Callum had been designated to accompany Grace to the hospital while his brothers and sisters dealt with things on-site. Wiley couldn't explain why he'd stalked to his car and followed the emergency vehicle, but he couldn't seem to release the impulse to be near Grace, even if she didn't want or need him there.

"You better hope she's okay," Wiley muttered.

Callum stopped directly in front of him, his eyes narrowing. "What's that supposed to mean?"

Wiley drew in a breath. How was he supposed to explain the fierce protectiveness he felt toward a woman he'd only just met? He didn't understand it, so there was no way his brother would.

"The hotel bears a responsibility for the accident. If the construction was faulty or the building materials subpar—"

"Are you kidding?" Callum's jaw tightened. "You know I don't cut corners, Wiley. Everything I build is rock solid."

"Other than the balcony that just collapsed with a woman standing on it." Wiley rose from his chair to stand toe-to-toe with his brother.

"I'm going to assume you're playing devil's advocate because you're an attorney and concerned about the family's liability. I sure as hell hope you aren't suggesting that we didn't take all the necessary steps to ensure proper construction." Temper flared between them, and Wiley wanted to kick himself in the family jewels for goading his brother at a time like this. The thought of Grace's injuries made him want to lash out at anyone and everyone.

He gave a tight nod. "I'm sorry, Callum. You're right. I'm worried about your employee and I'm concerned about the hotel's responsibility and the potential negative press of this kind of accident. There's no doubt about the quality of the work you do. I don't want a single incident to tarnish your track record in town."

Callum eyed him for a moment longer, then stepped away and began to pace again. "We won't let it. Of course we'll take care of any medical bills that aren't covered by Grace's insurance and continue to pay her salary while she's recovering. Once she returns to work—"

"You don't even know the extent of her injuries," Wiley felt compelled to point out.

"I can help with that."

They both turned as a tall man in light blue scrubs entered the waiting room. Callum strode forward and shook the man's hand, reminding Wiley of his brother's ties to the town.

"Mark, how is she?"

The man threw a glance in Wiley's direction.

"This is my brother Wiley. He's in town for Larkin's party."

"Quite an event," the other man murmured, which to Wiley's mind was the understatement of the new year.

"Wiley, this is Dr. Mark Matthews." Callum gestured to the doctor. "Becky says he's one of the best emergency room physicians she knows." He turned his attention fully to Mark. "I'm glad you're on duty tonight. How is Grace?"

"Good, given what she's been through." The doctor looked past Callum and Wiley to the empty waiting room. "Have you called her family?"

Callum nodded. "Ashley tracked down her parents' number and spoke to her mom. They're on their way here."

"Can we see her?" Wiley demanded, crossing his arms over his chest when both men gave him a strange look.

"I suppose that would be all right," Mark agreed almost reluctantly. "We've moved her to a room on the third floor for the night."

"How bad are the injuries?" Callum asked as Dr. Matthews turned toward a bank of elevators.

"You're not family, so I can't share any details." Mark jabbed at the elevator's button. "Grace will decide what she wants to tell you. She was awake when I left, but if she's fallen back asleep I don't want you to wake her. She's in room three sixty-five. I need to check on another patient, and then I'll be up."

Callum nodded. "Thanks, Mark. We won't disturb her if she's resting."

The elevator doors swished open as the doctor turned away. Wiley followed his brother into the small space.

"I appreciate you being here," Callum said as he

pushed the button for the third floor. "But you don't have to go with me to see her."

Wiley kept his gaze on the carpeted floor. "I'll stay."

He could feel Callum studying him but didn't answer. Let his brother think that his interest in Grace Williams was due to concern over the hotel's liability for the accident.

It made sense, and not only because of Wiley's career as an attorney. He'd never gotten particularly involved in the details of the lives of his siblings, at least as much as he could help it. After years of being part of such a large family, his identity as a separate individual meant the world to him.

He couldn't figure out why Grace had changed that in a split second, and he wasn't ready to examine it now.

Grace glanced up at the soft knock on the hospital door. Her head felt heavy and somewhat muddled, but now that the pain medicine had kicked in, at least her entire body no longer throbbed in agony.

She expected to see her parents' familiar faces. Shock rippled through her as Callum Fortune entered. She couldn't imagine that the man responsible for the construction of most of the new buildings in Rambling Rose would be too happy that one of his employees had managed to get herself practically killed in the middle of an important family event.

"Hey there," Callum said gently as he came closer to the bed. "Are you up for a couple of visitors?"

Her gaze moved beyond his broad frame and shivers erupted along her skin as she met the intense gaze of the man who'd captured her attention just before the balcony collapsed. Grace stifled a giggle that she knew must be caused by the pain medicine at the thought that her body's overwhelming reaction to Wiley might have caused the earth to move under her feet.

"Grace?" Callum gave her a strange look, and for an instant she worried she'd been singing the words to the classic tune out loud.

She swallowed and tried to pull together her tangled musings. "Thanks for stopping by," she said, and immediately thought she sounded ridiculous. As if Callum Fortune had come to her hospital room for some kind of social call. "I'm sorry I broke your balcony." Her voice sounded strange to her ears, thick and garbled.

Callum shook his head. "You didn't do anything wrong," he assured her. "There's no reason to be sorry. I'm the one who owes you an apology, Grace. I don't understand how or why that balcony collapsed. The county building inspector was out before the holidays and we passed everything."

Wiley stepped forward, clearing his throat. "We're glad you're okay."

The gentle gleam in Wiley's brown eyes made her

stomach flutter once again. When they'd been introduced, his eyes had appeared regular brown, but as
he approached the bed she could see flecks of gold
in their depths. His lashes were also outrageously
long for a man. Cosmetics companies could build
entire ad campaigns around the promise of achiev-
ing lashes like his.

She blinked and tried to focus, realizing she was
staring at him like some cow-eyed teenager. "Hi,"
she breathed, unable to form a more coherent greeting.

"Hello, Grace," he said, lifting her hand and
squeezing her fingers with what felt like something
close to admiration.

She'd always hated her plain, one-syllable name,
but on Wiley's lips it sounded like a poem.

"Hi," she repeated and felt color heating her
cheeks. Too bad she couldn't blame the pain medicine for her reaction to him.

"How are you?" he asked, like he truly cared
about her answer and not just her physical injuries.

"Did you two know each other before the party?"
Callum interrupted before she could answer, sounding both confused and irritated.

Oh, I know this man, Grace thought to herself. At
least she wanted to know him.

Wiley abruptly released Grace's hand. Immediately she wanted to reach for him again. Something

flashed in his eyes, and she had the thought that he might feel the same as her.

He broke eye contact with her to glance at his brother. "No. You introduced us."

"That's what I thought," Callum said, his voice flat.

Grace forced herself to focus on Callum. "I know the accident wasn't your fault, Callum. I—"

"Someone is sure as hell to blame."

She winced and brought a hand to her head at her brother's overly loud words. Jake and her parents hurried into the room, crowding around her bedside as the Fortune brothers stepped back.

Grace closed her eyes and wished for everyone to disappear other than Wiley. She wanted him to hold her hand again and ask how she was. She wanted to tell him she felt better when he was with her, even though that didn't make any sense. Still, it felt totally justifiable to her heart.

"Jake, this isn't the time." Grace opened her eyes as her mother placed a gentle hand on her brother's arm. "Our focus right now is Grace."

Her brother, older by two years, crossed his arms over his chest. "We can all agree that she wouldn't be fighting for her life in this hospital bed if it weren't for the shoddy construction at the hotel."

"I'm not fighting for my life," Grace said, lifting a hand to cover her mouth when another bubble of laughter threatened to escape. Her brother had always had a quick temper, but she sobered as she noted the look of consternation that crossed Callum's features.

"Oh, sweetheart." Her mother let out a soft sob, and regret pricked at the hazy fog filling Grace's mind. The last thing she wanted was to upset her mother. "We were so worried when that Fortune woman called."

Grace searched her brain for the details the doctor had shared about the extent of her injuries. "I'm okay, Mom. I broke my ankle and have a minor concussion."

Barbara Williams gasped. "A head injury?"

"Minor," Grace assured her, remembering the weeks after Jake's car accident when he'd lain in a medically induced coma while they waited for the brain swelling to subside. "Plus a few bruises and scrapes. Everything else came back clear."

"Are you sure?" her father asked, his tone gruff. Grace knew that rough exterior hid the heart of a teddy bear.

Her parents turned as Dr. Matthews entered the room. "She's sure. Grace was incredibly lucky that her injuries weren't worse. We're going to keep her overnight for observation due to the concussion, but we anticipate a straightforward recovery."

"Thank God." Her mother leaned forward to brush a kiss across Grace's forehead. "My sweet baby."

"I'm not a baby," Grace muttered. Even the cloud of fogginess from the pain medicine couldn't dull the annoyance at her mother's pronouncement, especially in front of Callum and Wiley.

Despite the caregiver role Grace had taken on during Jake's convalescence and the fact that she'd been managing her own life for years, her mom and dad continued to treat her like a dependent little girl. She tried to be patient with them, because she knew how much Jake's accident had made them aware of the mortality of their children.

Things had only been exacerbated when Grace moved back to Rambling Rose after the debacle at Cowboy Country. But her duties at the hotel gave her a sense of purpose and a feeling of independence once again. Now it felt like everything was in jeopardy.

Dr. Matthews frowned as she swiped a hand across her cheek, obviously misinterpreting the reason for her unwelcome tears. Grace didn't care what had caused the balcony's collapse, assuming nothing like that happened again. She did worry about what her recovery might mean for her future.

"That doesn't change the fact that someone is responsible for my sister being hurt." Jake shifted his glare between Callum and Wiley.

Callum's mouth thinned. "The hotel will take care of any medical expenses not covered by insurance.

Our priority is that she feels better as quickly as possible."

"To cover your assets," Jake muttered.

"Not at all," Callum countered.

"Do you really need to have this discussion in front of Grace?" the doctor asked impatiently.

"Or at all?" Grace added. She sent a beseeching glance toward her brother, silently pleading with him to give it a rest, but Jake only shook his head.

"You want to step out into the hall for a moment?" he asked Callum.

"Good idea," Callum agreed, and turned for the door.

Grace reached for her father's hand. "Don't let Jake be rude, Dad. This wasn't Callum's fault. The Fortunes aren't to blame. I know it."

A muscle ticked in Mike Williams's bearded jaw. Her father retained the stocky build he'd had as younger man, and added a few inches of girth around the waist. "I'll try to keep him calm." He patted the top of Grace's hand. "We're glad you're okay, baby girl."

Her stomach knotted as she watched her father follow the two younger men out into the hall.

Dr. Matthews gave her an encouraging smile. "You doing okay?"

"Fine," she murmured.

Her mom began to pepper the doctor with a litany of questions about her injuries and a recovery plan. Grace hated that she was causing her family this kind of worry or that she could be seen as a burden to the hotel.

"That 'fine' didn't seem convincing," Wiley said as he lowered himself into the chair next to her bed and scooted closer. "You're going to be okay, Grace. I promise."

She automatically smoothed a hand over her hair as if she had a reason to worry about looking pretty for Wiley Fortune. He was so close she could reach out and touch him. The urge was both overwhelming and nonsensical.

"You don't owe me any promises," she said instead, working to keep her wits about her despite the pounding of her heart and the effects of the pain medicine.

"I get that." He offered a tentative smile. "I can't seem to help myself."

She blinked and then looked away, wondering if he was truly as sincere as he seemed. Her mother was still talking with the doctor, nodding furiously and taking notes on a small pad of paper she'd pulled from her purse as he spoke in hushed tones. Her father had closed the door behind him when he'd ventured into the hallway. Grace had a feeling Jake was giving Callum all kinds of trouble, and she wished she could make it stop.

"My brother is protective," she told Wiley. "I'm

sure he'll realize that the balcony collapse was an unfortunate accident. Not anyone's fault."

"It's good that you have people to look out for you," he said.

"I guess you're right." She ran a finger along the edge of the thin blanket that covered her. "Although at the moment, I wish Jake would back off. I do want you to know that his accusations aren't personal. He doesn't have it in for your family or anything like that."

"Good to know." Wiley studied her for a long moment and then lifted his hand like he might touch her. With a shake of his head he drew it back again, and disappointment pounded through Grace.

"Do you have any other brothers or sisters?" he asked.

She got the impression he was trying to distract her from worrying about what kind of scene might be unfolding in the hall.

"No." She flashed a smile. "We're a small family compared to yours."

"Nothing wrong with that." He returned her smile. "What about a boyfriend?"

She felt her mouth drop open, and he immediately rose from the chair. He scrubbed a hand over his jaw, looking uncomfortable. "I'm sorry. Forget I asked that. It's none of my business."

"No boyfriend," she told him quietly, feeling heat rise to her cheeks. "My focus right now is the training program at the hotel." She wiggled her toes, which stuck out of the cast on her left leg that stopped just below her knee. "This couldn't have come at a worse time."

"Is there ever a good time to be standing on a balcony when it collapses?" Wiley asked, smiling again. Teasing her. Possibly even flirting with her?

Before Grace had a chance to process that, her father and Callum reentered the room.

Her mother took a step away from the doctor and frowned. "Where's Jake?"

"I sent him home," Grace's father said with a small shake of his head.

Callum's cheeks were flushed, his jaw taut. He motioned to Wiley. "We should go."

Grace sat up straighter on the bed. She wanted to protest Wiley leaving, but that would be stupid.

"Thank you for being here with me." She looked to Callum first before turning her attention to Wiley. "It helped a lot."

"I'm glad," he said, and the intensity in his gaze made it feel like they were the only two people in the room.

"Grace, I can't tell you how sorry we are that you were hurt tonight." Callum's commanding tone forced her to return her gaze to him. "Like I said earlier, anything you need, our family will take care of it. Just focus on getting well again."

"And back to work," she added quickly. "I want

to get back to work as soon as possible. Please let everyone know that."

Callum smiled tightly. "Of course."

"Work is the last thing you need to be concerned with right now," her father said with a sniff. He gave Callum a sidelong glass. "I want confirmation that your hotel is safe before I let my little girl go back there."

Grace bit back a frustrated groan. Was her father trying to make the Fortunes angry? Her potential future at the hotel meant everything. She wouldn't let anything—not even a collapsing balcony—jeopardize that.

"I understand, sir," Callum answered, but she could see by the set of his shoulders that it bothered him to have his workmanship called into question.

"It's fine." Wiley said, moving close to her again. His fingers brushed the top of her cast and despite the layers of plaster, she felt the touch like he was caressing her skin. "Callum understands that your family is upset. I'll talk to him."

"Thank you," she whispered, and bit down on the inside of her cheek to stem her tears. She didn't want to start sobbing in front of the two Fortunes on top of everything else.

Wiley thanked the doctor and offered a heartfelt reassurance to her parents, then followed Callum out of the room.

"I'll give you all a few minutes," Dr. Matthews said, "and then we can talk about next steps."

When the door closed behind the doctor, Grace let the tears flow.

"Oh, sweetie." Barbara was at her bedside in an instant. "You must have been terrified."

Grace took the tissue her mother handed her and blew her nose. "It happened so fast I barely had time to be scared."

"The point is it never should have happened in the first place," her father said, crossing his arms over his meaty chest. "What the hell kind of karma are we saddled with, Gracie, that we almost lose your brother and now you?"

"You didn't almost lose me, Dad."

"A second-floor balcony collapsed with you standing on it," Mike reminded her—as if she needed reminding. "You're very lucky."

"I know." Grace crumpled the tissue. "My injuries aren't anywhere near what Jake went through. I don't want either of you to worry about my recovery process. I'm going to get back to normal sooner than later."

"You can't rush it," her mother said, smoothing the hair from her forehead. "Let me get you a mirror and a wet towel. I'm sure you want to fix your face a bit."

Grace lifted a hand to her cheek. Fix her face? What was wrong with her face?

"You'll move home, of course." Her father's tone brooked no argument.

Grace argued, anyway. "I love my apartment, Dad. I can recover there just as easily." In truth, she didn't exactly love the cramped walk-up she'd rented when she returned to Rambling Rose, but it was better than moving back in with her parents.

Her father snorted. "You live on the second floor of a building with a staircase so narrow I can't believe it's even up to code. No way can you manage that with a cast."

"I could try," she insisted, even though she knew her dad was right.

"Grace Elizabeth."

She resisted the urge to roll her eyes but knew she had little chance of winning an argument when he used her middle name, as well.

"I appreciate the offer," she said instead. "It would make things easier until I'm out of the cast." Her parents lived in a quiet section of Rambling Rose in the same house Grace had grown up in. The house, a rancher, wasn't big, but it did have plenty of space for her.

"We'll take care of packing your things," her mother said, returning from the bathroom with a small handheld mirror and a stack of wet paper towels. "All you need to focus on is resting."

And returning to work, Grace thought to herself.

No point in saying the words out loud and engaging in another argument with her parents.

She took the mirror and a paper towel from her mom. "Oh, no." She glanced up and met her mother's concerned gaze. "Why didn't you tell me?"

"You'll clean up in a jiffy," Barbara said brightly.

All Grace could think about was Wiley seeing her like this. The cast was one thing, but her face was a mess. It wasn't injured—for that she was grateful—but she looked like she'd been on a three-day bender. Her hair hung limp around her shoulders and stuck to her head in several places. Her skin was pasty and pale, and the mascara she'd carefully applied before the event was puddled under her eyes.

If she had any question as to whether Wiley Fortune had been interested in her or simply concerned about her being injured at his family's hotel, she was fairly certain her appearance answered it.

Her ruined makeup and the ruined evening seemed to be par for the course in Grace's life. Finally things had been turning around for her, and then something had to happen to send her veering off her chosen path once again.

She began to wipe her face as she listened to her parents make plans for her unexpected homecoming. Grace couldn't help but wonder if she'd ever truly attain the future she wanted so badly.

Chapter Three

"That was sure as hell a shock."

Wiley turned as Steven approached from one of the hotel's patio doors. His brother kicked a small piece of terra-cotta-colored stone as he walked toward Wiley.

It was nearly nine on the morning after the party. Wiley wanted to survey the balcony rubble in the daylight and had held out an odd kind of hope that things wouldn't seem as bad in the aftermath of the accident.

Instead, they were worse.

The balcony's deck had ripped off the exterior wall, sending thousands of pounds of concrete and metal plummeting to the ground. Grace had fallen a good twenty-five feet, and it was truly a miracle she hadn't been hurt worse.

He said as much to his brother, who nodded. "Callum said she was in good spirits at the hospital. You were there with him, right?"

Wiley nodded. "She was also doped up on painkillers," he muttered. "I'm not sure we should judge her feelings about the accident based on last night, especially not if her family has any influence on her opinion."

Steven nodded. The two of them had an unspoken language. Wiley had been a toddler when their mother married David Fortune, who'd quickly adopted both of his new wife's young sons and given them his name. Wiley was close to all of his siblings, but he and Steven had a special bond.

Steven had been a committed bachelor until he'd met and fallen for Ellie Hernandez, the mayor of Rambling Rose. Things had started off rocky between them, but they'd quickly fallen deeply in love. Another Fortune who found his perfect future in this small Texas town. "That's to be expected, but we're all committed to doing the right thing by Grace. She's been a huge asset to the hotel. I know Nicole and Mariana feel the same."

"She's special," Wiley said as his gaze zeroed in on a flash of silver under a pile of debris.

"That's an odd description coming from you. I

didn't realize you and Grace had met before last night."

He could feel Steven studying him but didn't meet his brother's gaze. "We hadn't." Wiley walked forward, carefully picking his way through the mess.

He wore dark jeans and a cotton sweater plus the cowboy boots the triplets had given him for Christmas. As a confirmed city slicker, Wiley felt a little strange sporting boots, but they seemed to be expected in Texas.

He bent down and pulled a high heel from the rubble. Clearly one of Grace's shoes. The image of her unconscious on the ground flashed in his mind again, and his chest clenched in response.

"What's the deal?" Steven asked, sounding both curious and concerned. "You went to the hospital with Callum, and he said you were acting strange. Now you look like you've seen a ghost. If you and Grace don't know each other, why are you—"

"She could have died," Wiley blurted out, then rolled his lips inward. He needed to get a handle on his emotions when it came to Grace Williams. He couldn't explain to his brother the connection he felt with her. It had been immediate and intense, like a bolt of lightning slamming through him. "She was injured in a fall at our family's hotel. The hotel that Fortune Brothers Construction built. We're responsible for her, Steven."

His brother's thick brows drew together. "Are you

thinking about our potential liability in the accident? Is Wiley the attorney making sure we cover our—"

They both turned when a feminine throat cleared. "Sorry to bother you, Steven." A woman walked toward them from the far side of the pool. She looked to be in her midtwenties and wore a pencil skirt and a silk blouse that made her seem a bit overdressed for a casual Sunday. "There's a reporter in the lobby asking to speak to the hotel manager." She tucked a perfect blond curl behind one ear. "If you'd like I can talk to him?"

Wiley frowned at the gleam in the woman's gaze. "Who are you?" he demanded, not bothering to gentle his tone. In the same way that he'd felt an immediate connection with Grace, he had an instant dislike of this woman.

She swallowed visibly, her gaze darting from Wiley to Steven, who'd pulled out his phone and was typing in a message.

"Jillian Steward," she said, clearing her throat. "I'm one of the management program trainees at the hotel. I have a background in public relations as well as hospitality at my last position, so I'm more than equipped to deal with the press. That's part of the role of whoever is promoted to the GM position."

Grace had mentioned something about the trainee program last night. She'd seemed worried about her job given the extent of her injuries. Did she suspect one of her coworkers was going to take advantage of her absence? Wiley didn't like the thought of that.

Steven nodded absently. "I texted Callum and Nicole, but if you want to—"

"I'll talk to the reporter," Wiley interrupted.

Jillian's lips tightened. "I don't mind."

"Someone in the family should handle the media," he said. "As hotel counsel, it makes sense that I act as spokesperson."

"Hotel counsel?" Steven whistled under his breath. "Another new development."

Wiley nodded and focused his attention on Jillian. "Would you please tell the reporter I'll be with him in a minute?"

"Sure." The woman flashed a cheery smile. "We won't let Grace's absence hold us back. If you need anything else—"

"We don't," Wiley told her.

"She's just doing her job," Steven said as Jillian disappeared into the hotel.

"It sounded to me like she was trying to encroach on Grace's role." Wiley drew in a calming breath. "I don't like the thought of someone taking advantage of the accident."

"It sounds to me like you have a lot of thoughts where Grace is concerned."

"I'm doing my job," Wiley shot back.

"As far as you being the hotel's counsel, obviously I'm all for it. You know we'd like you to stick around Rambling Rose longer. In fact, weren't you scheduled to fly back to Chicago this afternoon?"

"I changed my ticket."

"Seriously?"

"Stop studying me like I'm some puzzle to figure out," Wiley grumbled. He didn't want to think that his brother could read the feelings he was trying to hide.

He'd texted his secretary early this morning asking her to change his airline reservation to give him a few extra days in Texas, mainly because he wanted to see for himself that Grace was doing okay. He wanted more than he cared to admit to see her again. No point in sharing those details with his brother. "The Hotel Fortune is a huge deal for the rest of you. That makes it a huge deal for me."

Steven's shoulders relaxed ever so slightly. "Thanks, Wi." He clapped Wiley on the back. "Appreciate you stepping in, even if it's temporary. I know that small-town life isn't your deal."

"Yeah." Wiley massaged a hand over the back of his neck. He would have agreed 100 percent with Steven's assessment before last night. Now he couldn't say for sure how he felt. "I'm going to go deal with this reporter. He won't be the only one interested in the accident. Let's plan to meet with everyone out at the ranch later and come up with some talking points going forward."

He nodded at his brother and then headed for the

front of the hotel, his mind wandering to Grace and when he might see her again.

Grace tossed her cell phone down on the hospital bed with more force than necessary. "You can't avoid me forever," she muttered, then glared at her cast leg.

She knew that everyone at the hotel was busy with preparations for the grand opening, but she'd called and texted Jillian Steward, her counterpart in the management program, a half dozen times and had yet to receive a response.

Grace and Jillian weren't the only two trainees, but they were the pair that had been singled out by the Fortunes to be considered for the promotion at the end of the six-month program. That meant Jillian was the competition, and Grace knew the woman would use every advantage she could to make herself seem more deserving of the general manger position.

And Grace was stuck in a hospital bed.

She'd received calls from a range of Fortunes since the accident, all of them conciliatory and thoughtful.

The family had sent an enormous bouquet of flowers. Grace appreciated the gesture, but when she'd asked about joining the regular Monday staff meeting by phone, Callum had told her that her only focus at the moment needed to be healing. She wondered if her mom had gotten to him.

"Who's avoiding you?"

Her gaze darted to the open door to find Wiley Fortune standing there, looking just as handsome as he had Saturday night. He wore dark jeans and a gray sweater that somehow made his brown eyes look even darker.

"No one important," she said, and offered him a weak smile, once again aware of the disparity in their appearances. She wore an old flannel shirt over her hospital gown. Although she'd managed a shower earlier with her mom's help, Grace hadn't bothered to apply makeup or do anything with her hair. She tucked a thick strand behind one ear, wishing she'd considered the possibility of a visitor she might want to impress.

"Are you up for some company?" he asked, almost hesitantly.

It was strange to see a man like Wiley appear anything but totally confident.

"I'd like that," she said, and he approached the bed. He'd been holding one hand behind his back and pulled it out to reveal an exquisite bouquet of flowers arranged in a beautiful cut-glass vase.

"These are for you." He gave a soft laugh. "Obviously."

"Thank you." She gestured him closer and sat up in the bed. "They're beautiful. Calla lilies are my favorite."

His smile widened. "You're just saying that to be nice."

"It's true," she assured him. "They remind me of summer."

"They reminded me of you," he told her. Something in the low rumble of his voice made goose bumps erupt along her skin.

She breathed in the sweet floral scent as he held the bouquet close to her. "Mine seem a bit small in comparison." He touched a finger to the enormous arrangement on her bedside table as he placed his vase next to it.

"The hotel sent those," she said. "Along with a fruit basket."

"Thoughtful," he murmured. "Everyone is relieved that you weren't hurt worse." His gaze clouded over as it roamed over the cast. "It could have been really bad."

"If I spent my time worried about things that could have happened, I'd never have the strength to get out of bed in the morning." She squeezed her hands together and focused on staying calm. "I would have given up a long time ago."

He sat down in the chair her mother had situated next to the bed. "You can't ever give up, Grace."

"I'll keep that in mind if I can convince my parents to stop coddling me." She didn't want to sound bitter but couldn't help her frustration. "I know I'm lucky, but what good does that do me if I lose my job at the hotel?"

Wiley frowned. "You aren't going to lose your job. They'll give you time to heal. Healing is your priority."

She let out a groan of frustration. "I'm so sick of hearing that," she all but shouted, then realized how she must sound when Wiley's eyes widened in shock.

"Are you sure we hadn't met before yesterday?" She shook her head. "Because I don't normally vent to people who are practically complete strangers."

"The first time I saw you was at the party," he said, his tone gentle. "That brief introduction wasn't enough, but I thought we'd have all night to talk. Then you walked out onto the balcony and…" He ran a hand through his hair and looked away. "I wish I wouldn't have left your side."

"You couldn't have known what would happen." She reached out and covered his hand with hers before thinking about what she was doing. For several seconds, they both stared at the place where they touched. Hers was paler and looked small against his larger, golden-hued skin.

"I still regret not being able to protect you."

"But if you'd been on the balcony we both would have been hurt." Her heart beat against her rib cage, and she drew back her hand. She liked touching Wiley way too much. "I don't need to be protected and am doing my best to convince my parents of that."

"Parents worry. It's part of the job description."

Something in his tone made her wonder what he wasn't saying. "Do you...um...have kids?"

"God, no." He held up his hands in protest, like she'd just asked if he had cooties. "No wife or girlfriend, either, for the record."

She laughed softly. "Thanks for sharing."

"I'm more the uncle versus father type. Some people just aren't cut out to be a parent, you know?"

"Some aren't cut out for monogamy, either," she countered. "Unfortunately, my last boyfriend was one of those."

Wiley cringed. "Sorry."

"Me, too."

He tapped a finger on the chair's wooden armrest. "People should know their limits. If a guy can't be committed, he shouldn't commit."

Grace wasn't sure how they'd gone down this path of conversation. But it was par for the course that she was harboring an unexpected attraction for a man who just admitted to basically being allergic to relationships.

"That's why my focus is my career," Grace said, then cleared her throat. Could she really claim a career after three months in a management training program? "My job at the hotel and the possible promotion after the grand opening. It's everything to me."

"That's right," Wiley said with a nod. "They're going to hire a general manager locally. I met someone else today who's part of the training program. Jillian something or other."

"Steward." Frustration balled in Grace's stomach. "Jillian Steward. She also wants the GM role, and I'm sure she's going to take advantage of me being on leave to ingratiate herself to everyone." She groaned out loud when Wiley shifted in his chair. "I'm sorry. I don't know why I'm sharing so many of my personal struggles with you. Jillian is a qualified candidate. Not more qualified than me, of course. Your brothers and sisters can make whatever decision they want about the promotion. I just hope I'm cleared to return to work sooner rather than later."

"My brothers and sisters think highly of you," he said with a sincere smile. "Missing a few weeks from work won't change that."

"Weeks?" She shook her head. "There's no way I'm waiting weeks. The hotel will practically be open by then. There's way too much to do and—" She paused, narrowed her eyes at Wiley. "Is that why you're here? Did they send you to tell me I can't come back until I'm done with the blasted cast? I know that's what my mom wants, but she's—"

Grace's mother entered the room, closing the door harder than she needed to. "Your mother has your well-being at the forefront of her mind. I'm sure Mr. Fortune would agree that your recovery is most important."

Wiley quickly stood and took a step away from

the bed. "Most important," he repeated, and Grace felt her lips twitch at how discombobulated he looked facing down her mother.

Barbara Williams was a petite woman, several inches shorter than Grace, with a delicate frame that belied her inner strength. She worked part-time at the high school library and had since Grace and Jake went to school there. Their mother claimed it kept her busy and out of her husband's hair. Unfortunately, when she arrived at the hospital this morning, she'd also announced she was taking a few weeks of unpaid leave until Grace was up and around.

Except Grace wasn't sure how that was supposed to happen while living under her mom's overprotective thumb.

"I assume that's why you're here," Barbara said to Wiley, her tone cool. "To assure Grace she has no worries about her position since she was injured on the job."

"I stopped by to…" Wiley scrubbed a hand over his jaw, the slight scratching sound doing funny things to Grace's insides. "That is to say I'm…"

"Why are you here?" Grace frowned at how flustered Wiley seemed. She certainly hoped that didn't mean his plan had actually been to give her some bad news about her job. When he'd walked in, she'd been so darn happy to see him that she hadn't bothered to question his appearance.

She couldn't deny the connection she'd felt with

him from the moment they locked eyes across the Roja banquet room. Given the invisible thread that apparently linked them together, it had seemed appropriate for him to visit her.

But her mother's skeptical gaze made Grace doubt what she felt.

If doubts were dollar bills, she'd be a millionaire.

"Your job is secure," he said, sounding less like the flirting man who'd entered her room and more like a stuffy attorney. The type of professional she'd come to distrust during her brother's fight to ensure that insurance paid his medical bills after the car accident.

Somehow those words did little to relieve her anxiety.

"Thanks for relaying that message," her mother said. "I'm sure the Fortunes who were responsible for the construction are far too busy trying to determine what went wrong to bother stopping by."

"Mom, stop. Callum called earlier and both Steven and Dillon as well as Nicole and Megan have texted. It's fine."

Her mother sniffed, then sent another glare in Wiley's direction.

"I should go," he said, offering Grace a wan smile. "I'm glad you're doing well, Grace, and hope you'll be out of the hospital soon."

"The doctor wants another round of concussion

testing before she's released." Barbara flung the words at Wiley like they were a personal accusation.

"Do they suspect things are worse?"

Grace wasn't sure what to make of the concern in his gaze, but it warmed her heart. Of course, it could just be that he didn't want his family on the hook for additional medical expenses. That's what her brother would say. Somehow, she didn't believe it.

"She's fine," her mother said before Grace could answer. "But this is really a situation for the people close to her to handle. Her family."

"I understand," Wiley said with a pinched smile. "Please let me know if there's anything I...any of us at the hotel can do to help."

His gaze darted to Grace and then back to her mother before he left the room.

As soon as he disappeared, Barbara began to flit about the room, clearly filled with agitation.

"Mom, you were so rude to him." Grace wanted to go after Wiley, but she couldn't do anything stuck in this bed. The crutches a nurse had brought in rested against the wall, but it would take far too much time to manage them.

"Why was he here, Gracie?" her mother demanded, clasping her hands tight in front of her like she had to hold them together to keep in her nervous energy.

"To check on me."

"That doesn't make sense. He barely knows you."

Grace had to agree that in theory it didn't make

sense, but her heart told her it was perfectly reasonable for Wiley to be at her side.

"He's being nice," she said, because explaining the feeling of connection she had with him would be a losing argument.

"Covering his family's assets is more like it."

"You sound like Jake." Her brother had visited earlier, railing about the hotel and rumors of shoddy construction he'd heard from friends around town after reports of the balcony collapse got out. Since Rambling Rose was such a tight-knit community, word spread fast. "What happened at the hotel was a freak accident. The Fortunes are good people, Mom. They've already done so much for the town."

Barbara's mouth thinned, but she nodded. "I agree, but buildings don't just fall apart for no reason. Jake feels that there's something suspicious about the balcony collapsing the way it did."

"Jake needs more hobbies," Grace grumbled. "Or to watch less true-crime television."

Her mother's features gentled. "You have a point, but the Fortunes have had problems in the past. I remember hearing about some crazy ex-wife causing all sorts of trouble for the family. There was even talk about a kidnapping."

"Those aren't the same Fortunes." Grace closed her eyes and silently counted to ten, hoping for patience. "It was Jerome Fortune—the tech giant who reinvented himself as Gerald Robinson—whose family had those issues. He eventually found happiness, though, with his first love. And Wiley's father, David, wasn't involved in any of that. The difficulties haven't followed the Fortunes to Rambling Rose as far as I've heard."

She wanted to strangle her brother for putting these doubts into her mother's head. Barbara had always been protective, but she'd become even more of a worrier after Jake's accident. The severity of his injuries and the fear of losing him had rocked their small family to its core. Grace knew her mother's fear had seeped into her consciousness, as well. It had made Grace hesitant about taking chances, and now that she was finally getting a shot at a real career at the Hotel Fortune, she wasn't going to let unfounded rumors derail her.

"I thought they were all related in some way."

Grace opened her eyes to see her mother studying Wiley's bouquet.

"Distantly," she agreed. "But Callum and his siblings weren't close to their cousins growing up. From everything I've learned working for the hotel, they moved here from Florida with the intent to establish themselves without significant ties to the rest of the Fortune family. No one is out to get them. Why would they be?"

"These are pretty," her mother said absently. "Calla lilies are your favorite."

"I know." Warmth infused Grace's chest once more as she thought about the fact that Wiley had somehow known her preference in flowers. "Mom, tell me you believe what I'm saying. I'm not in danger working at the hotel."

"I believe the Fortunes mean well," her mother conceded. "At first, I was skeptical of the scope of their plan for the town. It felt like a bit of an invasion to those of us who grew up here and were happy with things the way they were."

"The town was dying, Mom."

"That's going a little far."

"But it's true. The Fortunes have attracted new residents and visitors from all over Texas and the surrounding states. Already-established local businesses have benefited, as well. Even the mayor agrees." Ellie Fortune Hernandez, the town's popular young mayor, had expressed doubts about Callum's plan at the start but had quickly come to be one of the Fortune family's staunchest supporters, in no small part thanks to falling in love with and ultimately marrying Steven. "And Mariana is helping with the hotel's signature restaurant. Everyone in town loves her for all those years she ran her famous market. If she's behind the project, we know it's in the town's best interest."

Her mother held up her hands, palms out. "Okay, Gracie. No need to take out a billboard to advertise all of the wonderful things the Fortunes have done in

Rambling Rose. I'm glad for the town to benefit from their efforts, but my main concern is you. It's all well and good for some new-to-town family to have success, but not if my baby is at risk because of it."

Grace blew out a frustrated breath. "I'm not at risk. And I'm going back to work as soon as the doctor tells me I can. This injury won't jeopardize my future."

"I heard Wiley say your position is secure."

"My current position," Grace clarified. "He has no control over the GM role, and he already hinted that Jillian was making a play for it. If she takes over my responsibilities while I'm out as well as handling her own, she could make a strong case for why she's the best candidate."

"There are plenty of places to work that don't involve the Fortunes," her mother said, even though they both knew that wasn't true. At least not places in Rambling Rose that offered Grace the opportunities she craved.

"Mom, I'm happy to be back here." She loved Rambling Rose but hated that she'd returned on the heels of her life imploding. It was why she was so determined to earn the GM position. "But I can only stay if I can make a future for myself. I feel like the Hotel Fortune is my best chance for that. My only chance right now. I need you to support me and to make sure Dad and Jake do, too."

Her mother sniffed. "Good luck with that."

"That's what I'm afraid of." Grace leaned forward and touched her cast, blinking away tears. "Please, Mom. I know you're worried, but this is important to me. After I found out about Craig cheating and resigned from Cowboy Country, it felt like I'd never have another chance to prove myself. I don't regret coming home from college after Jake's accident, but my life veered off path after that. I want a course correction. I need it."

"Oh, Gracie." Her mother lowered herself to the edge of the bed and put her arms around Grace's shoulders. "You know I support you. Your dad and your brother, too, in their own way. We all just want what's best for you."

Sloppy tears flowed down Grace's cheeks, and she didn't try to stop them. She'd tried for the past twenty-four hours to put on a brave face, but so much felt out of her control.

After a minute, she pulled back. She hated that her mother was crying, as well. There had been so many tears during Jake's recovery. Grace didn't want to be the cause of any more. "I don't know what's best," she admitted. "But I do know what feels right, and the hotel is a big part of that for me." She wiped the cuff of her flannel shirt across her mom's cheeks, earning a watery smile. "I trust the Fortunes, especially Wiley. I can't explain it, but there's something about him."

"Well, he's quite handsome." Barbara skimmed

her thumbs over Grace's cheeks. "He has a very cute butt."

"Mom." Grace laughed. "That's pretty bold."

"I might be middle-aged, but I'm not dead."

Grace hugged her mom again, then blew out a shuddery breath. "It's more than how he looks. It's how he looks at me. Like I'm special."

"You are special. But—"

"I know nothing will come of it," Grace said quickly, embarrassed that she admitted so much to her mom. "He was only in town for the birthday party, and I understand he's checking on me because he's an attorney and he's worried about the family's liability. That's how lawyers are."

A part of her hoped her mother would argue, but Barbara nodded. "Smart girl. Keep your wits about you when it comes to men who seem too good to be true. I remember how fast you fell for Craig."

Grace frowned, not sure how to explain that her connection to Wiley felt different from anything she'd experienced before. Why bother? Chances were she'd never see him again, anyway. She pressed her fingers to her chest and tried to rub away the sudden pinch.

"Will you help me convince Dad and Jake not to make trouble with the Fortunes?"

Barbara looked away for a long moment but finally nodded. "I'm not quite convinced, but you deserve happiness. As long as you follow the doctor's orders and don't push yourself too much, I'll support you."

Grace smiled. "Thank you, Mom. I promise I'll take care."

Chapter Four

Wiley sat at the empty Roja bar the following evening, sipping a scotch as he stared out the patio doors to the rubble of the collapsed balcony. Callum's crew would begin cleanup and new construction tomorrow morning. Although the mess was both an eyesore and, more importantly, a reminder of the accident, they'd had to wait until the insurance adjuster and building inspector gave them the go-ahead.

Unfortunately, the inspector's report had been both better and worse than any of them could have imagined. Better because the man verified that the accident hadn't been a result of shoddy workmanship. Worse because his finding indicated that the support beams had possibly been tampered with, rendering them structurally unsafe and likely the cause of the collapse.

"Mind if I join you?" Nicole asked as she approached from the restaurant's kitchen. She wore a white chef's coat and dark pants, her mass of thick hair pulled back into a tight bun. The restaurant had been open on select weekends but wouldn't expand its hours until the following month when the hotel officially opened. Nicole spent as much time on-site as their brothers, working on Roja's menu and training the staff. Sometimes it still shocked Wiley to see his baby sisters functioning as capable adults. He'd left for college when the triplets were still in middle school. While he'd been home for vacations and holidays, he hadn't paid much attention to the fact that Nicole, Ashley and Megan had grown up while he was away living his life.

"It's your liquor," he told her, gesturing to the bottle.

She scrunched up her nose. "I'm going to have a glass of wine."

"I'll take a glass of what Wiley's offering." Callum appeared in the doorway, his brows drawn together and stress lines bracketing either side of his mouth.

Wiley imagined he looked just as tense. Nicole did, as well. They hadn't shared the news of potential sabotage with anyone outside the family yet, but it was only a matter of time until the information leaked. Wiley wasn't sure what made him angrier, the idea that Grace had been hurt by some unknown adversary or that other employees at the hotel might still be at risk.

"We don't have enemies," Callum said as if reading Wiley's thoughts. He took a seat on the plush leather bar stool next to Wiley, and Nicole handed him a glass. "I know the deputy raised questions based on the report, but it isn't true."

He poured himself a generous amount of scotch, then refilled Wiley's glass.

"Are you sure?" Wiley demanded.

"What other explanation could there be?" Nicole added as she came around the bar and sat on Wiley's other side.

"I don't know," Callum admitted. Wiley understood how much it took for his capable brother to say those words out loud.

"You told me that people around here weren't thrilled with your plans for the hotel." Wiley sipped the scotch, the dark liquor doing very little to warm him.

"We handled it." Callum nodded like he was trying to convince all of them. "Kane was instrumental in helping smooth things over. We got input from a whole cross section of the community and implemented their ideas into the design. As far as we've heard since then, everyone is behind the project. People understand that the hotel will benefit local businesses across the board, not just the ones we own."

Nicole twirled her wineglass between two fingers. "Do either of you think it was strange that the officer asked about the situation with Gerald Robinson and his ex-wife?"

"The evil ex-wife," Callum muttered.

"Charlotte," Wiley said. "I didn't know the details, so I did a little digging this afternoon and called Dad to see what he remembered about her case."

"Dad and I were together at the wedding when Charlotte tried to kidnap one of the guests." Callum drew in a deep breath. "That woman was definitely trouble."

Wiley wiped a droplet of condensation from the rim of his glass. "It wasn't just the attempted kidnapping. Charlotte burned down Gerald's house and caused all kinds of trouble. She was off the rails."

"But she's in a psychiatric hospital now," Callum said.

"And why would she want to harm any of us?" Nicole asked. "Dad isn't even close to his half brothers, and we have very little contact with that branch of the family. The Austin Fortunes I've met are nice, but it's a stretch to think anyone from their world has a grudge against us."

Wiley nodded. "I agree, but it would be nice if discovering the culprit could be cut-and-dried or if we could say for certain that whatever happened with the beams was a onetime accident. At this point, the idea that someone wants to sabotage us and not knowing who or why isn't doing much for my peace of mind."

"Imagine how the rest of us feel," Callum said. "You're upset, and you don't have anything at stake in this venture. If we don't get a handle on what might be happening, I could lose everything."

Wiley's blood pressure spiked at his brother's words. He knew Callum was right in a business sense, but Wiley did have something to lose. Someone, anyway.

He'd heard that Grace had been discharged yesterday after his visit. While he was happy to know she was well enough to go home, he didn't know what to do with his strong desire to see her again. He couldn't very well just show up at her parents' house without a good reason.

He also couldn't seem to stop thinking about her. No point in explaining the attraction to his brother when Wiley still didn't understand it himself.

"We're going to make sure that doesn't happen," he promised.

Callum gave him a curious look. "What are you planning to do from Chicago?"

"I'm actually thinking of staying on in Rambling Rose until the hotel opens next month." He said the words calmly, hoping neither of his siblings would question him.

"Wi, that would be amazing." Nicole set her

wineglass on the glossy bar top and threw her arms around him. "It will be like old times with all of us together. You're the last holdout, you know."

Callum clasped his shoulder. "Are you sure?"

"I talked to the senior partner today and confirmed that I can work remotely for a few weeks. I'll still have to give time to my clients. We're working on closing a huge deal with a manufacturing company, but I should be able to manage it. That way I can also help with whatever needs to be done around here." Thinking about having a purpose made him feel calmer. "I'd like to review the employment contracts and insurance policies for the various ventures in town to make sure everything is in good shape."

"Sounds great," Callum told him.

"I'd also like to talk to some of the employees," Wiley said.

Nicole gasped softly. "You aren't suggesting that someone who works for us was involved with the balcony?" She shook her head. "This is a tight community, Wiley. It's not like the big city where people are out for themselves. Like Callum said, we got people to support the hotel. I don't want to even consider that anyone would want to do us harm."

"I hope you're right." Wiley drained his glass and then stood. "But one of your employees was injured in that balcony collapse. Grace could have died."

His sister's blue eyes filled with tears, and she glanced away. "I know."

"Don't get upset." Wiley wanted to kick himself and even more so when Callum's fingers tightened around his scotch glass. The last thing he should be doing was making his siblings feel bad. They had the best intentions when it came to their plan for Rambling Rose. He knew that.

"I don't believe for a minute that anyone working for the hotel was involved," Callum said. "Fortune Brothers Construction has never dealt with sabotage, but I know of contractors who've had their sites vandalized and projects derailed. Sometimes the motivation is as simple as someone looking for attention."

Wiley nodded. "The reporter I talked to yesterday was from the local paper, but that doesn't mean the story won't be picked up by news outlets in bigger cities around Texas if it's a slow news cycle."

"I hate having our business out there for public consumption." A muscle ticked in Callum's jaw. Wiley could feel the anger and frustration radiating from both his brother and sister. He wanted to find a way to ease their anxiety, however he could manage it.

"The paper here comes out weekly, right?"

Nicole nodded.

"Hopefully," Wiley said, clasping his hands together in front of his chest, "this incident will have blown over by the time the story runs. We should come up with an event to bring some positive publicity to the hotel before the grand opening. Show the town that the Fortunes are here for the long haul and dedicated to doing what's right for Rambling Rose."

Callum and Nicole both expressed their agreement with his idea. Nicole pulled out her phone. "Grace would have been our go-to for a community event. She has a way with people."

The understatement of the century, as far as Wiley was concerned.

"We'll have to ask Jillian to take the lead. I can text her tonight and then schedule a meeting with her and the other trainees tomorrow for—"

"No." Wiley stepped forward quickly and held up a hand. "We should let Grace handle this if she's up for it."

He kept his features neutral as his brother and sister stared at him in disbelief.

"You must be joking," Callum said finally. "She was the one hurt in the accident. Why would we ask her to coordinate a publicity event in response?"

"She called earlier today," Nicole added, "and said that she's staying with her parents while her leg heals. They're encouraging her to rest and recuperate for at least a few weeks. Of course I told her that she can take all the time she needs, so I can't very well turn around and push her to return to work right away."

"I know what her parents want," Wiley said, thinking of Grace's distress in the hospital. "But do you think she agrees? When I talked to her, she was eager to return to work."

"When did you talk to her?" Callum's tone was suddenly suspicious.

"In the hospital," Wiley said with a wave of his hand. "You know that." He hadn't told anyone about his visit to her the previous day.

"She was loopy on pain medicine." Callum shook his head. "We can't trust anything she said that night."

"We should at least ask her." Wiley pointed at Callum. "As for why, the reason should be obvious." And it had nothing to do with Wiley's desire to spend more time with her, or at least that's what he wanted to believe. "If the employee who was injured is the one representing the hotel, that shows her faith in the family and the Hotel Fortune. You can't buy that kind of press."

"Good point," Callum agreed.

Nicole didn't look convinced, but she nodded. "I don't want to bother her at night. I'll call her in the morning and ask, but I won't pressure her."

"Let me talk to her," Wiley offered with what he hoped was a reassuring smile. "Since she was such an integral part of the team before the accident, I'd love to ask if she noticed anything suspicious before Larkin's birthday. I can mention the idea of an event and see what she thinks."

"I'm not sure," Nicole said, her tone hesitant. "She barely knows you."

Exactly, Wiley thought to himself. He needed an excuse to spend time with her. Maybe that would quench the thirst he had deep in his soul when it came to Grace. "She won't think I have an ulterior motive with regards to her job security."

Callum barked out a rough laugh. "You're an attorney. She'll think you have an ulterior motive. Your profession isn't known for rampant altruism."

"Thanks for the vote of confidence," Wiley grumbled. "Come on, Callum. I want to help while I'm here, and I'm here until all of this gets settled." He turned his attention to his sister. "I promise I'll be nice to Grace and make sure she knows her healing is our top priority. At least let me start the conversation with her. If it doesn't go well, you can take over."

Nicole looked like she wanted to argue, then glanced at Callum. "We're overextended as it is. If Wiley wants to talk to Grace, I guess that would be okay. But being nice is no joke."

"Nicole is right." Callum leveled him with a steely stare. "Don't go corporate attorney and terrify her or offend her family. The whole point of the hotel's training program is to generate goodwill within the community by offering opportunities to Rambling Rose locals, and now one of them has been hurt on the job. Any way you look at it, the situation is a PR nightmare. We have to keep Grace happy."

Wiley wasn't about to go into all the ways he wanted to keep Grace happy. "I understand," he said, hoping his expression didn't give away the anticipation building inside him now that he had a reason to visit her. "Nicole, would you text me her parents' address? I'll stop by tomorrow and then check in with you both and let you know how it went."

He said goodbye and headed for his car. All he could think about was the impending visit to Grace's house and how he couldn't wait to be near her again.

Grace sat on the overstuffed couch in her parents' cozy family room the following morning, staring at the book in her hand and realizing she'd read the same page three times. With a groan, she flung the paperback across the room. It slammed into the wall and dropped with a thud to the floor just as her mother appeared in the doorway.

"I guess you're not a fan of romance novels," Barbara said with a shake of her head. "Grace, if you're done with the outburst, you have a visitor."

"Sorry," Grace muttered. "I just hate lying around like this. I feel so useless." She raised a brow when she finally met her mother's gentle gaze. Barbara's cheeks were flushed, and she worried her hands in front of her. "What is it? Who's here, Mom?"

Her mother glanced over her shoulder in the direction of the front hall and gestured the visitor forward. "It's…um…"

"Hello, Grace." Wiley came to stand next to her mom. "I apologize for not calling first. It actually didn't cross my mind until your mom answered the door. If this isn't a good time…"

"It… No…this is…great…fine… I'm happy to… It's fine…" She started to straighten, nervous energy scrambling her brain cells. Wiley Fortune, the man who had consumed her thoughts since he'd walked out of her hospital room two days earlier, had come to see her. He was standing in her parents' modest house, staring at her like—well, like she was someone special.

"Grace appreciates you stopping by," her mother said, the corner of her mouth twitching.

Realizing she wasn't going anywhere gracefully with the cast, Grace settled back onto the cushions and offered Wiley a friendly smile. She hoped it came off as friendly and not deranged, although he made her feel just a touch unbalanced. "What she said," Grace muttered.

Barbara picked up the book Grace had thrown against the wall and handed it to Wiley. "Have a seat," she told him. "I'll check on the two of you in a bit. Would you like a glass of iced tea, Wiley?"

"Yes, ma'am. Thank you."

Color crept up Barbara's cheeks as Wiley focused his attention on her. *See, Mom*, Grace thought. *You can be suspicious all you want, but a man that handsome is hard to resist.*

When her mother disappeared toward the kitchen, Wiley took another step into the room, glancing down at the book he held.

"Don't you dare make fun," Grace said, tugging on the hem of the Rambling Rose High School sweatshirt she wore. She hadn't dressed expecting visitors. Her parents had grabbed a random assortment of clothes from her apartment, so this morning Grace had thrown on an old high school sweatshirt and a pair of baggy sweatpants after cutting off one leg at the knee. Now she wished she'd thought to dab on a bit of lip gloss or at least a spritz of perfume.

"I wouldn't dream of it," Wiley promised. "I assume the duke mentioned in the title would be the brawny man on the cover."

"You'd assume correctly."

"I never imagined old-time aristocrats to be gym rats—" He held up the book and tapped a finger on one of the duke's broad shoulders "—but this one is quite the impressive physical specimen."

"He fences and boxes," Grace said, hiding her smile.

"Ah." Wiley placed the book on the coffee table. "That explains it. Although not why I heard the book crashing against the wall when I arrived. Too much throwing punches and not enough wooing for your taste?"

"Plenty of wooing," she confirmed. "But I'm already sick of sitting around." She reached out a hand

and brushed an invisible crumb off the cast. "I'm going to go crazy by the time my ankle heals."

Wiley offered her a smile so sweet it made her knees go weak. "We'll make sure that doesn't happen," he promised.

Grace desperately wanted to believe Wiley. Still her family's warnings ricocheted through her brain, and she told herself not to be taken in by his charm. Was that even possible? "Shouldn't you be back in Chicago?"

He lowered himself into the chair beside the couch, and she tried to see her parents' house through his eyes. It looked much the same as it had when she'd been a kid, with wood-paneled walls, bookshelves filled with family photos and her father's collection of historical nonfiction books.

"I've decided to stay in Rambling Rose until the hotel opens."

She tried to keep her features neutral even as excitement spiraled through her. Did that mean he wanted to see her more over the next few weeks? She should know better than to read too much into the way he looked at her, but she couldn't seem to stop her body's reaction to the intensity of his gaze.

"I'm sure that makes your brothers and sisters happy."

"For now." He laughed softly. "I'm going to make sure everything is in order with employment agreements and contracts for the various businesses they've gotten involved in. They'll be happy to have me here unless it makes more work for them."

"I doubt that. I can tell from seeing them interact at the hotel that your family is really close."

"They are," he murmured.

"Why doesn't it sound like you include yourself in that 'they'?"

He shrugged. "I've always been a sort of odd man out when it comes to our branch of the Fortune family. For me, it was important to feel like I'm making my own way, which is why I left Florida for college and didn't return even after law school. I wanted my life to be my own."

"I know how that feels." She swallowed back the emotion that clogged her throat. "You're lucky you've been able to accomplish it."

"Lucky," he repeated, then frowned. "I suppose you're right."

A few seconds of silence descended between them, and although it was weighted, the quiet didn't feel uncomfortable. In fact, Grace's chest loosened as she drew in air laced with Wiley's spicy scent.

She snapped back to attention at the sound of a bag crinkling. Her eyes had zeroed in on his handsome face, and she hadn't even seen the sack he held.

"I didn't come here to bore you with my family dynamics." Wiley flashed a self-deprecating smile. "I'm here to deliver a get-well care package."

"You've already brought me flowers."

One thick brow arched. "Is there a limit on the number of gifts I'm allowed to bring you?"

She wanted to laugh at the absurdity of that question. "I'm not going to put one on you." She reached for the bag he now held out. "I'm just not used to being on the receiving end of so much generosity." She inwardly cringed, embarrassed to admit she was comparing Wiley to her ex-boyfriend. Craig had been steady and reliable—or so she'd thought—but never the romantic type.

Grace had convinced herself she didn't care. She thought it was important to have a man she could build a life with, not someone who lavished her with gifts and romantic gestures. She got enough of that vicariously through books and movies.

As she peeked in the brown paper bag with the Hotel Fortune logo stamped on the outside, she tried to remember that Wiley was just being nice because she was a hotel employee. His brothers and sisters were all busy with preparations for the opening and taking care of their other businesses in town. Chances were good that they'd designated him as the family liaison for the injured employee. At least that's what Grace's brother would tell her.

She put aside thoughts of her ankle and her brother as she pulled out a stack of puzzles, a candle and a box of chocolates. "How thoughtful. I love all of it. You didn't have to…" She glanced up at him as she continued to remove items from the seemingly bottomless bag. "Did you buy one of everything in the hotel gift shop?"

Wiley scrubbed a hand over the back of his neck. "Just about. I didn't know what type of games you might like, so I got word searches, sudoku and cross-word puzzles."

"I like word searches," she told him with a smile.

He nodded. "They had both dark chocolate and milk, and I can tell you my sisters are very specific with their chocolate, so I got a box of each."

"I like both." She held up two candles.

"They both smelled good," he said, sounding almost embarrassed that he'd packed so much into the bag. "But not as good as you. You smell like a spring rain shower." He gave her a sheepish smile. "Do I sound like a sad imitation of your romance duke?"

"No, but for the record I smell like water," she said with a laugh, then reached out and patted Wiley's leg when he frowned. "I'm joking. The lotion I use is actually named Rainforest Mist so you're right on the money with that."

Wiley's eyes darkened even more and the space between them seemed to shift—growing thick with a yearning that Grace didn't understand, although it sent shivers rippling along her skin.

"Thank you," she managed after a weighted moment. "I appreciate all of this and you coming to see me. I haven't reached out to many friends because I don't want to talk about the accident. People are so curious, and I just want to forget."

There was an immediate shift in Wiley, as if she'd just doused him with a bucket of icy water. "I figured people would be talking to you about the incident. In fact, a reporter came by the hotel on Sunday. The local paper is doing an article on the circumstances of the accident."

The thought of having her name associated with the event that was bringing the hotel bad publicity made Grace's stomach clench, but she nodded. "He reached out to me, as well. He wants to interview me for the story."

"Are you going to talk to him?"

She shrugged. "I guess I should, but I'm not ready yet. Don't worry, though. I'll be sure to make it clear that the hotel had nothing to do with the balcony's collapse."

"You don't have to do that. We appreciate your loyalty, Grace, but you can speak freely."

"I know," she whispered, distressed by the formality that had seeped into his tone. "But it's true. Obviously, I wish it wouldn't have happened, but the hotel isn't responsible."

His opened his mouth as if to deny her claim, then closed it again. "Speaking of the hotel…" He flashed a smile that was different from the one he'd given her before. It didn't reach his eyes. "I do have a speck of official business to discuss with you."

"Sure." Grace ignored her disappointment and reminded herself that she could read whatever she wanted into the way Wiley looked at her. That didn't make the promise in his gaze something real.

"Callum, Nicole and I talked about coordinating a small community event before the official grand opening. Nothing elaborate or time-consuming for the staff, but something that would…"

"Make people forget that I could have died in the balcony collapse?"

He blew out a shaky breath. "Yes."

She nodded, appreciating that he didn't try to sugarcoat the motivation. There was nothing wrong with what the hotel wanted to do. The Fortunes were running a business, and they needed positive PR. They couldn't run a successful hotel without paying customers. If the hotel didn't make money, Grace wouldn't have to worry whether her injury would prevent her from earning the promotion. There would be no promotion to be had.

"It's a great idea." She sat forward on the sofa, lifting her cast leg and placing her foot on the floor. The doctor had told her it was important to elevate the leg, but somehow she felt too much like a blushing maiden from one of her historical romances sprawled out on her parents' sofa as she and Wiley discussed actual business. Grace was thrilled to talk about something other than the accident, even if she wasn't officially on the clock. "I'd actually recomm cusing on other local business owners. We should also involve the spa and Provisions. Nicole and Roja can provide the food—samplings from the regular menu. I bet even the vet clinic could set up a booth in conjunction with a local animal rescue. It's important to remind the community leaders how much your family has already contributed to the town and give a glimpse of how good it's going to be. A Rambling Rose partnership would benefit everyone."

"Those are great suggestions."

Grace held up a hand. "I'm not done." She shifted again, wishing she could get up and pace as she worked through the possibilities in her head. Her crutches rested against the stone fireplace on the wall across from the seating arrangement, but she didn't want to bother with hopping over to retrieve them. Plus, she'd look like a complete fool trying to pace using crutches. For what felt like the millionth time since Saturday night, she cursed that blasted fall.

"Tell me more." Wiley reached out and squeezed her hand, as if he could sense her frustration. His touch had the immediate effect of calming her, and she drew in a breath before continuing.

"We want Rambling Rose businesess to feel connected to the hotel. Do you think your brothers and sisters would consider offering a 'locals' weekend'?"

"Um…probably."

She clapped her hands together. "I should have thought of that even before the accident. The hotel can give a discounted rate for a particular weekend, one during a slow season where occupancy would naturally be down. They'd get the great deal if they booked during the reception, and we could do a raffle for a free dinner for two at Roja." She paused and scrunched up her nose. "I keep saying 'we,' but I mean 'you' obviously. The Fortunes and the employees who are actually working. I'm sure other people will have ideas, as well." Jillian, Grace thought inwardly, would have plenty.

"Are you interested in the 'we' part?" Wiley asked and, once more, Grace's brain seemed to short-circuit. All she could think about was a "we" that involved her and Wiley. She was interested like nobody's business.

"Yes," she managed, hoping he assumed she was talking about being engaged on a professional level.

"There's no pressure, of course." He smiled at her again, encouraging and warm, and she felt it all the way to her toes. "I'm being nice, right?"

She frowned. "Is that a trick question?"

"Nicole warned me I had to be nice," he said with another laugh. "Callum told me not to act like an attorney."

"I actually haven't been thinking about you being an attorney during this visit," she admitted. "If that helps."

"Good." He nodded. "If you think you're up for it, we'd like you to handle the reception. You can take care of a lot of the planning from here. Whatever works best for your recovery. Obviously, you're qualified based on the rush of ideas you just offered. Getting more buy-in from local business owners makes sense to me, although you'll have to run that focus by my siblings. Again, only if you feel like it wouldn't be too much."

"No." She tried to breathe around the knot that had formed in her chest. This was her dream come true as far as the scenario for the weeks of her recovery.

"No, you're not up for it?" His brows drew together.

"No, it's not too much. I'd love to be involved in any capacity. If you feel like I can handle it, then absolutely yes. I'd love it."

"Absolutely not."

At the sound of the booming male voice, Grace glanced at the door to find her father standing next to her mother, his arms crossed over his chest in a stance Grace knew all too well. Barbara held a tray with iced tea glasses and a bowl of pretzels. The look she threw Grace was both resigned and apologetic.

This would be a battle, and it was one she didn't intend to lose.

Chapter Five

Wiley stood as Grace's father entered the room. "Hello, sir. Grace and I were just discussing—"

"She's not going back." Mike narrowed his eyes at Wiley, then switched his glare to Grace. "You aren't going back."

"Dad, I'm a grown woman." She made to stand, but her cast hit the edge of the coffee table, and she sat back down, wincing as pain radiated up her leg.

Her mother let out a gasp, and Wiley reached for her.

"Don't touch my daughter." Her father's voice seemed to reverberate through the room.

Grace felt her face color with humiliation as Wiley drew back his hand and took a step away from her. Barbara put the tray of drinks and snacks on a side table and moved closer to her husband. Grace wasn't sure if it was to lend silent support to Mike or to protect Wiley from him.

"I'm sorry, Mr. Williams. I just wanted to help."

"By putting her at risk again? Not going to happen."

"I want to work." She lifted her hands, palms up. "I can't sit around here for the next month. I'll go stir-crazy." She bit down on the inside of her cheek when her voice caught. No way was she going to start crying in front of Wiley.

"Did he tell you that someone's out to get the Fortunes?" Mike asked Grace the question but looked at Wiley as he spat out the words.

"What are you talking about?"

"Sabotage." Mike said the word like it was poison on his tongue.

"We don't know that yet," Wiley argued, then turned to Grace. "The building inspector said it's possible someone tampered with the balcony's support beams. The investigation is ongoing, but that could have contributed to the collapse."

"Definitely is more like it," her father said. "Why is someone messing with the hotel construction?" he demanded of Wiley.

"We don't know, sir." Wiley scrubbed a hand over his jaw. "But I promise you we'll get to the bottom of it."

"Not by making my daughter a potential target."

"I promise I would never—" Wiley cleared his throat. "I won't let anything happen to Grace. I'll keep her safe. You have my word." He turned to her fully, and her breath caught in her throat at the ferocity in his gaze. "I'll keep you safe."

"I know," she said softly. Somehow she had no doubt that Wiley, a man she barely knew, would do everything in his power to ensure her safety. It baffled her why she felt so confident in that, but her heart remained certain.

"He's using you," her father said through clenched teeth.

"Mike, don't." To Grace's surprise, her mother stepped forward and placed a hand on her husband's arm. "What happened to Grace was an accident. The Fortunes didn't intentionally put her in danger. I agree that she should take it easy." Barbara glanced at Grace. "You need to rest so that your recovery isn't impacted."

Grace opened her mouth to argue, but her mother held up a hand.

"I also understand that you're accustomed to being busy, and your job means a lot to you." She squeezed Mike's arm. "She's an adult capable of making her own decisions."

"I know what I'm doing," Grace said, looking between her parents. "Going back to work will actually be helpful to my recovery." She ignored her dad's snort of disbelief. "I mean it. I can't do nothing for a month. If the Fortunes are willing to let me make my own hours and work remotely when possible—"

"We are." Wiley nodded. "Whatever you need."

"I want to try." She got to her feet again, this time careful about her leg, and hopped the short distance to where her parents stood. "I understand you're worried, and I have no idea who would want to sabotage the hotel or why. But it has nothing to do with me."

"You've got a cast on your leg that tells a different story," Mike said, but his voice had gentled. Grace knew he wasn't going to fight her on this any longer.

"I'll be careful."

Mike turned to Wiley. "My daughter is old enough and smart enough to make her own decisions. But I'm holding you to the promise to keep her safe. I understand you don't have skin in the game in Rambling Rose the way some of your brothers and sisters do, but consider my girl your number one priority while you're in town."

"Dad, that's ridiculous." Grace cringed even as longing threaded through her like a needle binding two pieces of fabric. What would it feel like to be a priority for Wiley? "Wiley has plenty of other—"

"Done," Wiley said, and held out a hand to Grace's father. They shook and suddenly Grace felt like some sort of Victorian spinster who'd just been promised to the roguish hero. She needed to lay off the historical romances for a while.

"Can Wiley and I have a few minutes alone?" she asked her parents. "To go over next steps."

Mike looked as though he didn't want to leave them, but Barbara tugged him toward the hall. "Let us know if you need anything. It was nice to see you again, Wiley."

"You as well, Mrs. Williams. Thank you."

When her parents were gone, Grace turned to Wiley, ready to give him a litany of excuses for her father's behavior. Instead an enormous yawn stretched her lips and exhaustion made her limbs grow heavy.

"This is too much," Wiley said without hesitation. "I promise that wasn't my intention, Grace. Or to upset your father."

She waved away his concern. "I'll be fine," she told him with a wobbly smile. "I probably need a tiny nap first. My dad's worry has more to do with what happened to my brother than this situation. Although I wish you would have told me about the possibility of the beams being tampered with."

"I'm sorry." He squeezed her fingers. "I should have brought it up right away but didn't want to upset or worry you. I meant what I said about protecting you, Grace."

"Thank you," she managed, even though her throat had gone dry. It was difficult to remember that her relationship with Wiley was only professional when he touched her with such exquisite sweetness and looked at her as though he wanted to kiss her. It had to be the exhaustion making her imagine that. "I appreciate the opportunity to coordinate an event for the hotel. I'm going to take a short rest, and then I'll put together my ideas and email them to Callum and Nicole. We can schedule a call to discuss their thoughts and go from there."

"All business," Wiley murmured, dropping his hand. If Grace didn't know better, she would have sworn she heard disappointment in his tone.

"Not all." She flashed a smile and gestured to the pile of puzzle books on the table. "You've given me a lot to keep myself busy. I appreciate it." She covered her mouth when another yawn escaped.

"We'll talk soon." Wiley stepped away from her. "Enjoy your nap, Grace. Sweet dreams."

Butterflies fluttered across her stomach as he walked away. If Wiley Fortune was a part of her dreams, they'd be sweet indeed.

"I'm still not sure why we couldn't have taken one of the ATVs," Wiley grumbled the following night as he tugged on the reins of his horse when the animal once again veered off the path to munch on a nearby bush.

"We wanted to give you the full Texas experience," Megan said, glancing over her shoulder with a wink.

"Besides, your boots are too shiny." Their cousin

Kane rode up next to him on his chestnut mare. "You need some more dust to make you look like a legit cowboy."

Wiley barked out a laugh at the absurdity of that statement. "I'm nowhere near a cowboy. Attorneys aren't cowboys. It's mutually exclusive."

"Not in Texas," Megan told him. Her horse came to a stop at the edge of a low rise, the surrounding property spread out in front of them like a postcard.

"How much of this do we own?" Wiley asked, somewhat overwhelmed by the wide-open space and big sky. He knew this part of Texas was expansive, especially compared to the crowded high-rises of downtown Chicago.

"As far as the eye can see," Megan told him softly. There was something about the moment and the vista that called for quiet. Wiley suddenly understood what had drawn his siblings to this part of the country. Maybe it was something in the Fortune DNA that made Texas appeal to so many of them.

He thought Callum had lost his mind when he'd moved to Rambling Rose over a year ago and then convinced Dillon, Steven and Stephanie to go with him. By the previous spring, the triplets had joined them. Wiley had stayed in the Midwest, telling himself he was content with his big-city life far away from his family. He loved each one of them, but growing up in a house with so many kids had made him savor his independence and stake it out with all the dedication of a dogged adventurer. His career and his life belonged solely to him, and that seemed like enough.

But spending time with his siblings and the cousins he was enjoying getting to know planted tiny seeds of doubt in his mind. Although he was keeping up on his regular workload remotely, he didn't miss the bustle of the city and his busy professional life the way he assumed he would. He'd been going on full tilt for as long as he could remember, never pausing to reflect whether the path he was so intent on taking was the right one.

Of course it was right. He'd chosen it. He couldn't let a few weeks of fresh air and the sweet smile of a woman derail him. Yes, it was fun to be involved in the family business, but that didn't mean it would be better to return to the life he knew.

"I'm happy for you guys." Wiley leaned forward and patted the horse's strong neck. "You all seem to have found your place here."

"It's an easy town to call home," Megan said, a trace of wistfulness in her voice. "Also easy for some people to find love, apparently."

Kane snorted, adjusting the brim of his hat. "You don't need love to be happy."

Wiley nodded. "Amen, cousin."

"You are two peas in a pod." Megan wrinkled her nose. "What do you have against falling in love?"

"Not a thing." Kane shrugged a big shoulder. "It's just not for me."

"Me, neither, yet," Megan conceded, "but I'm not opposed to Mr. Right walking into my life. The hotel is going to open right around Valentine's Day. Wouldn't it be nice to have a romantic date with the perfect girl to share it with?"

An image of Grace popped into Wiley's brain, and he shifted in the saddle. "I think we need to keep our focus on making sure the grand opening goes off without any more problems. That's way more important than romance."

Kane nodded, a muscle ticking in his jaw. "I'd feel a lot more confident if we could get to the bottom of whether or not someone tampered with the balcony's support beams."

"I want to believe there's some explanation for the collapse." Megan blew out a frustrated sigh. "It's too scary to think that someone has it out for us or that we might be putting our employees or potential customers in danger." She adjusted one of her stirrups and glanced between Wiley and Kane. "Everything is going so well with the businesses, especially Provisions. The reservation book is filled almost every night, and the online reviews are excellent. I know Roja will be just as much of a success, assuming nothing else happens."

"It won't," Kane promised. Their cousin was taking the lead on hotel security, and Wiley had been impressed with his attention to detail.

"How do you know?"

"I met with a security company earlier today," Kane confided. "Another firm is coming in to look over the property tomorrow. I'm going to fast-track the process of getting bids so that we can have an updated system installed by the grand opening. There won't be any loose ends."

"I've started meeting with employees," Wiley said. "Everyone seems positive so far. No hint of discontent, which is good. It could be that the balcony was just a fluke or someone looking for attention."

"I hope you're right." Megan gave her horse a soft kiss, and the animal turned toward the path again. She met Wiley's gaze as she passed him, and he hated the anxiety in her cornflower blue eyes. All the brothers were protective of the triplets. He wanted his sisters to be able to focus on the positive aspects of their new business ventures without worrying about potential sabotage.

Wiley brought his horse abreast of hers. "It's going to be okay, Meggie."

"You make me believe that." She gave him a warm smile. "It's your commanding attorney presence. I was on the call with Grace this morning. We video-conferenced, and it was the first time I'd seen her since the accident. She looked good."

"What did you expect?"

"I'm not sure," she admitted. "I thought maybe she'd seem bitter or angry that she was dealing with a broken ankle."

"Grace has always struck me as a practical girl," Kane called from behind them. "All of the trainees are great, but she shines under pressure."

"Pressure is one thing," Megan answered. "Falling from the second story of the hotel is quite another."

"True," Kane admitted tightly. Wiley knew the accident weighed heavily on everyone's mind.

"How did the call go?" he asked, trying to sound casual. "I felt bad that I couldn't be a part of it, but a client meeting came up that my assistant wasn't able to reschedule."

"It's fine," Megan told him. "We appreciate you pitching in here while managing your regular life at the same time. No doubt you'll be glad when the hotel opens, and you can be rid of us and our troubles for a while."

"You aren't a trouble," he told her.

"That's nice." She laughed. "But you aren't fooling me, Wi. I remember how crazy our full house drove you when we were younger. You'd hide in the basement with the water heater just to get a little privacy."

"Nothing wrong with a teenage boy wanting privacy," he muttered, earning a loud chuckle from his cousin. He leveled a stare at Kane over his shoulder. "Not for the reasons you're thinking."

"Gross." Megan snorted. "Enough about teenage boys and privacy. The call went well. Grace put together a really comprehensive time frame and plan for a preopening reception aimed at local business leaders. We're going to suggest a Rambling Rose partnership, where restaurants, shops and other local businesses actively work to promote each other. It's a short turnaround, with her idea to put the event on the calendar for the last week of January, but it will be a perfect lead-up to the grand opening."

"Her parents are worried that she's going to do too much and compromise her recovery." A knot formed in his stomach as he recalled the look her father had given him, like Wiley was the lowest form of scum he could imagine. Wiley prided himself on his moral compass but should probably to do a little more research into the accident Grace's brother had a few years ago.

He could tell by the comments Grace made that Jake's situation had impacted everyone in the Williams family, and he wanted to understand how traumatic it had been for them.

"We won't let that happen," Megan said as the horses approached the barn at the ranch. "You won't let that happen."

He arched a brow and kept his features bland, hoping to hide the thrill of anticipation that pulsed inside him. Keeping an eye on Grace was the easiest assignment he could imagine.

"I mean it, Wiley." The three of them dismounted, and Megan wagged a finger at him. "We're counting on you to take care of her."

"Not exactly a chore," Kane said as he took the reins of Wiley's horse and started toward the barn. "Grace is fantastic."

Wiley didn't like the bolt of jealousy that zipped through him at his cousin's words. He had no reason to believe Kane had designs on Grace. They worked together, just like she and Wiley did. Ugh. That thought didn't make him feel any better.

"I'll make sure she's taken care of," he told his sister as they followed Kane into the barn, reminding himself to keep his attraction to her under control. It would be best for everyone involved—but more difficult for him than anyone would imagine.

Chapter Six

Grace sat on the porch swing looking out over her parents' front yard the next day. Her leg was elevated and her other foot bare as she swung gently in the cool afternoon air.

She'd had to put on a heavy jacket, but it was worth it to escape her mother's fussing, her father's silent admonishment and her brother's outright agitation at the fact that she was already back to work less than a week after the accident.

The doctor had told her to take recovery at her own pace, she'd reminded them, and she was being careful not to spend too much time on the phone or at the computer. She'd even napped for an hour after lunch, even though it frustrated her how weak she still felt compared to her normal energy level. Grace liked moving and working. From the time she'd gotten her first babysitting job as a teenager, the ability to make her own money and her way in the world had always appealed to her. Her parents had provided a great life for Jake and her, but finances had always been tight. As a girl, she remembered hearing her parents argue about the monthly budget. Her father had a tendency to spend beyond their means, a constant source of worry for Grace's mom.

Grace had grown up with the deep desire to never be a burden on anyone. She knew Jake felt the same, and that was part of the reason why his accident had been so difficult. His recovery had taken months and had been a challenge for every member of their close-knit family.

That didn't make it any easier to hear him degrade Wiley and the Fortunes. The hotel was one of the best things that had happened to Rambling Rose, and certainly for Grace, so she was already tired of having to defend her employer.

She blew out a breath and hit Send on the email she'd just written to Nicole, making suggestions of potential offerings for the business reception that would showcase Roja's planned menu. The Fortune triplets certainly had a way with food, and Grace envied their confidence and the bond they obviously shared. She'd met their other sister, Stephanie, as well, and although she wasn't involved in the hospitality industry, she was helping to coordinate a booth for the local vet clinic where she worked.

Grace waved as Collin Waldon walked across her lawn from his father's house next door.

"Tell me you're not posting cast selfies on social media," he called to her.

Collin was as close as Grace got to having a second brother. They had been tight friends since she could remember. Her mother loved to trot out photos of Grace and Collin playing together in the plastic baby pool in their diapers, and Grace knew that her parents and Collin's father, Sam, still held a secret hope that the two of them would eventually end up together.

The idea of a match between them was comical. It would be like dating her brother, although she couldn't deny that Collin had grown into an insanely handsome man. He was tall with a lean build, dark hair and coppery eyes with gorgeous light brown skin. As a captain in the army, he was currently stationed in Germany. His years in the military had honed his body into a network of hard planes and muscles.

"I'm working," she told him, then glanced toward the house. "As well as getting a much-needed break from my family."

"Jake said you weren't going back to the hotel." Collin climbed the porch steps two at a time.

Grace growled and made a face. "Jake is even

worse than Dad right now. He's not the boss of me, and it's high time he figures that out."

"Aw, Gracie, he means well."

"Don't even go there, Collin." She wagged a finger in his direction. "You're my friend, so you have to be on my side."

"Always." He rested a hip against the porch railing. "But you can't believe that your parents and Jake aren't on your side. They love you."

"I know." She blew out a frustrated breath. As aggravated as she was by her family's fussing, she knew everything they did was motivated by love. "But I want to work, and I love my job at the hotel. I'd love it even more if they made me general manager when the hotel opens. I've worked so hard, Collin. I need a chance to prove myself."

"Even if the hotel is being targeted?" He raised a challenging brow.

"Jake needs to stop spreading rumors," she muttered.

"You could have died, Grace."

"Why does everyone keep reminding me of that?" She slammed her laptop closed, once again cursing the cast and her limited mobility. There was no way she could stomp off the way she wanted. As soon as the blasted cast was off, Grace would never take walking freely for granted again.

That thought took the wind out of her sails of righteous anger in an instant. Of course Jake and her parents were extra worried and overprotective. He'd battled back after the accident, working with physical therapists and doctors and on his own for months in order to walk again. Yes, Grace had left college and come home to help, but no one could understand what Jake had been through during that time other than him. She had no doubt the accident and the ensuing long, painful recovery and legal fight over responsibility had changed her once happy-go-lucky brother.

Now she was annoyed by not being able to walk across the front porch without her crutches. She rubbed a hand over the top of her leg and nodded at Collin. "I understand how bad the accident could have been, and I appreciate my family. But I told myself when I came back to Rambling Rose that I was going to find a way to have the life I wanted, to go after my dreams and not let anyone stand in my way."

Collin frowned. "Are you talking about your jerkwad ex-boyfriend?"

"Maybe," Grace admitted. "We both worked at Cowboy Country, but I did my job and helped him with his. Did I tell you he got a promotion based off a marketing plan I basically wrote for him?"

"Five minutes alone in a room with him," Collin said with a dark laugh. "That's all I need."

"You sound like my brother," she told him, shaking her head.

"Great minds."

"I'm happy to be back to work, and I can't wait until I feel strong enough to go into the hotel and have my social life back, too." She held up a hand when her friend would have argued. "I'll be safe there, Collin."

He shifted to sit more fully on the porch rail. "How do you know?"

Wiley's handsome face appeared in her mind. "I just do. You should come by and check it out. The restaurant is going to be fantastic. I know you appreciate a good kitchen."

"Yeah." He nodded. "My dad doesn't exactly have gourmet tastes."

"How's he doing?" Grace knew it hadn't been Collin's plan to return to their small hometown, but when his father had taken a turn for the worse after Collin's stepmother passed away, he'd come back. Although not officially related, Grace and Collin had the family-duty gene in common.

"He seems okay since I've been here, but I've don't have a lot of leave time. I'm still worried about how out of sorts he's been since my stepmom died."

"He loved Sharon very much," Grace said gently. "I'm sure having you here on leave helps him feel better. I only wish you could stay longer."

They both glanced toward the street as a sleek black sedan pulled up to the curb. Grace's heart fluttered against her ribs when Wiley climbed out of the vehicle. He wore a crisp white button-down shirt and dark pants with aviator sunglasses covering his brown eyes.

"What were you saying about a social life, Gracie?" Collin lifted a brow. "Because you're blushing at the stranger in the fancy clothes."

"Shut up, Collin." Grace returned the wave Wiley gave her as he approached the house. "He's not a stranger. He's a Fortune."

Collin elbowed her. "Well, isn't that interesting."

"Not to you," she muttered.

"Hello, Grace." Wiley glanced between her and Collin. "You look well."

It was kind of crazy how two words—*hello, Grace*—could cause a riot of sensation to pulse through her body every time he said them.

"I'm working." She held up her laptop. "On plans for the reception. It's coming along really well. I'm well, too, of course. Just like you said."

Collin straightened from the porch rail and leaned in. "You're babbling."

"Go away, Collin."

He threw back his head and laughed. As much as he was annoying her in this moment, it was good to hear him laugh. He'd done far too little of it since returning home.

Collin gave the swing a little push, then turned to Wiley. "Collin Waldon," he said, holding out his hand. "I'm a good friend of Grace's."

Wiley's chest expanded as he nodded. "I'm Wiley Fortune. Grace and I—"

"Are working together on the hotel event," Grace said, planting her foot on the wood porch to stop the swing. "In fact, we're discussing plans this afternoon. Collin was just leaving."

Her childhood friend grinned at her over his shoulder. "I'll talk to you later, Gracie."

She shifted on the porch swing as Collin headed back to his father's house, moving her cast leg to the ground.

"Would you like to sit down?" She patted the cushion next to her and offered a smile.

"Does he live next door?" Wiley asked as he moved toward her.

A shallow line of tension had appeared between his brows.

"Since we were babies," she confirmed. "We grew up together—best friends for as long as I can remember. Collin's in town on leave to visit his dad. He's been in the army for years."

Wiley took a seat next to her. "And now you're staying with your parents. How convenient for catching up."

She glanced at him from the corner of her eye. If Grace didn't know better, she'd think Wiley sounded jealous of Collin. A thrill passed through her at the thought of that. She really didn't want the attraction she felt for the handsome attorney to be completely one-sided.

"Collin's a good guy," she said, and maybe she kept her phrasing slightly cryptic just to gauge Wiley's reaction.

She wasn't disappointed. His jaw tightened for several seconds before he finally turned to her with a smile that was patently forced. "It's important to have good friends in your life."

"Yeah." She tried to keep her mouth from twitching in amusement, but Wiley's gaze narrowed on her.

"What's funny?"

"Nothing. I'm just happy to see you."

He visibly relaxed at her words. "I didn't really come here to discuss the hotel event. Although I'm happy to talk about it if you want. Nicole and Megan said you're doing an amazing job already."

Pride blossomed in her chest at the praise. "We're just getting started, and I still wish I was coordinating everything on-site. I hope by next week I'll feel strong enough to come to work at the hotel."

"That's great." A breeze blew a few curls across Grace's face and before she could push them away, Wiley reached out and with a gentle touch, tucked her hair behind one ear. "You have the most beautiful hair."

She swallowed back a nervous giggle. "I used to hate having wavy hair. When I was growing up, the popular style was sleek and straight. No matter how much product I used, mine would never behave. But I've gotten used to it, although it's a rat's nest when I wake up." She raised a hand to her mouth when she realized she was babbling again, but Wiley didn't seem to notice.

"I'm sure it's beautiful in the morning, too."

The rough timbre of his voice tickled her skin as she thought about waking up with a man like him next to her. Good Lord, that would be something special.

She cleared her throat and gave herself a mental "down, girl" command. "If you aren't here to talk about the event, is there something else? Do you have more information on who was behind the balcony collapse?"

"I wish I could say I did. Not yet, though. I stopped by to... I wanted to see you."

Oh.

Grace felt heat flame her cheeks. Wiley Fortune wanted to see her. She could definitely get used to that.

A tapping sound came from the house, and she turned to see her mother standing at the living room window looking out at them. Grace suddenly felt like she was a teenager again with her nosy parents trying to insert themselves into her business. Wiley waved at her mother, who returned the wave and gave him a beaming smile. At least her mother was being friendly. Grace didn't want to think about what would happen when her dad realized Wiley was here.

"Would you like to go for a drive?" She stood as she asked the question.

"Sure," he answered, quickly straightening to join her. "If you have time?"

She hopped toward the front door, laptop tucked under her arm. "All the time in the world. Just give me a minute to tell Mom I'm leaving and grab my shoes and crutches." She didn't really like using them, so she typically hopped around her parents' house.

"I'll be here."

Great. Wiley would be waiting for her.

Her mother opened the door as she reached for the handle. "Wiley is here," she stage-whispered.

"Yes, I saw you watching us from the window."

Barbara winced. "Sorry. That was too much."

"It's fine. We're going for a drive." Grace made her way past her mom and gently closed the door. "Can you grab my crutches from the family room?"

"Where are you driving to?" Her mother placed a hand on her arm. "Do you need something, sweetie? Your dad is in the garage. He'd be happy to get you—"

"Wiley came to see me." Grace covered her mother's hand with her own. "Not to talk about work or the balcony. To see me."

Her mother's mouth formed into a small O.

"Exactly." Grace bit down on her lower lip. "We're going for a drive. I don't know where." She checked her watch. "Maybe out for dinner. Maybe…it's a date."

"I'll get the crutches," her mother said with an enthusiastic nod. She gently pinched Grace's cheeks and smoothed a hand over her hair. "There now. You look so pretty with a little color in your face."

"Mom, have you become a Fortune fan?" Grace asked as she bent to retrieve her shoes—or shoe—from under the front table.

"I'm a fan of seeing my daughter happy," Barbara said. "You look happy for the first time in a while, sweetie."

"Thanks, Mom."

With a nod, her mother headed down the hall while Grace sat on the chair in the foyer and tied the laces of her sneaker. They weren't the most exciting choice in footwear, but she was still getting used to the crutches. Better to be practical than wind up on her back end in front of Wiley.

She glanced at the front door while she waited for her mom. It was probably rude to leave him standing out there, but Grace had needed a minute to compose herself. He'd said he wanted to see her. It wasn't some grand profession of devotion, despite the way her heart reacted. Other than his family, he probably didn't have many friends in town. Maybe he was just bored, and she was a distraction.

A short-term distraction, she reminded herself, even though her body ignored the warning. Her mother was right. Grace hadn't felt this excited in a long time.

Her mother returned with the crutches. "Have a good time on the drive or dinner or whatever you do."

Whatever. Grace couldn't even entertain the possibilities of "whatever." Not with her leg in a cast and her mother standing next to her. She grabbed the crutches and smiled. "I appreciate that," she told her mom, then scrunched up her nose. "I'd also appreciate if you not mention it to Dad or Jake—"

"Go have fun with your friend." Barbara reached around her to open the door. "Your dad and brother don't need any details."

Wiley turned as Grace hopped out and closed the door behind her. She arranged the crutches under her arms and started forward. "Sorry about the wait."

"No problem." He glanced between her and the porch steps. "But speaking of problems…"

"I can manage." She gave him a bright smile. Okay, so she hadn't actually dealt with steps other than when she'd returned from the hospital, but she would make it work. "I appreciate you taking me out for a bit." She got to the top step and handed him the crutches. "Could you hold these for a moment?"

"Of course. Are you sure you can manage it?"

No. "Yes."

"I could help you…"

"I've got it." Grace was probably a fool for refusing an excuse to get close to Wiley, but she wanted to prove to herself that she could handle a flight of stairs on her own—even if it was just five wooden porch steps. If she was going to head back to work the following week, she'd need to get a lot more proficient at moving around on her own.

She grabbed hold of the railing for support and hopped down each step, proud when she didn't once lose her balance. "I didn't fall," she announced with a wide smile as he returned the crutches.

"You did great." He looked at her with a huge smile.

"That was silly," she said as they started down the walk toward his car. "Maneuvering down a few steps isn't a big deal, but this is the farthest I've gone on my own since the accident. If my parents had their way, they'd encase me in Bubble Wrap for the rest of my life to make sure I stayed safe."

"It's an understandable sentiment from people who care about you."

"But not what I want."

He opened the car door for her, and she gave him the crutches to stow in the back seat. The whole process was slow and awkward. By the time Grace was buckled in next to Wiley, sweat dripped between her shoulder blades, and she felt like she'd run a marathon. How could less than a week of inactivity make her feel like such an invalid?

As if sensing her frustration, Wiley placed a gentle hand on her arm. "You've been through a lot, Grace. Your ankle and the cast are the biggest outward signs of the accident, but you fell from the second story."

She offered a wan smile. "I have the bruises to prove it."

"Give yourself a bit of...well, grace."

"I never thought of attorneys as naturally comforting people," she admitted. "But you're good at giving support."

"It's a hidden skill." He released her hand and pulled away from the curb. "We lawyers don't like to let anyone know about our human side. It ruins the reputation of being coldhearted, and then people aren't afraid of us."

"You're the opposite of scary."

"Where are we headed?" he asked when he got to the stop sign at the end of the block.

"The highway," she said without hesitation. "As much as I love Rambling Rose, I need a break. Let's get out of this town, Wiley."

Chapter Seven

Wiley sensed the change in Grace as they cruised down the open road. She'd given him directions to the highway, and they were headed west out of Rambling Rose, destination unknown—at least to Wiley. He liked giving control to Grace. Wiley's life was normally a rigid list of schedules and meetings, so the idea of not having to worry about anything for an evening was strangely liberating.

The sun was just beginning to set, and fluffy clouds filled the sky overhead, swaths of cotton candy against the blue of the sky.

He couldn't explain how right it felt to have Grace next to him, to finally be alone with her, even on a drive to nowhere special. He wanted to make whatever time they spent together special. She deserved that, and he had a primal urge to be the man to give it to her.

Tiny remnants of jealousy still quivered in his stomach, out of character for him. Even when he dated, Wiley had never been the jealous type, but seeing Collin Waldon lean close to Grace had made him want to lose his mind. She'd described him as a friend, but their connection was obvious. What man in his right mind wouldn't want more from Grace?

Wiley certainly did.

"I love this time of day," she murmured, splaying her hand against the passenger window. "It's amazing how we take for granted the little things in the hustle and hurry of regular life. I never thought about it being a treat to leave the house whenever I wanted."

"I'm honored to be the one to help you escape," he told her with a wink. Open pastures and fields filled with herds of cattle glided by on either side of the highway. Similar to the trail ride with Megan and Kane, this drive gave him another glimpse into the Texas landscape, and the sheer scope and size of it gave him an unexpected sense of peace. How was it that a self-described city slicker could feel such a connection with wide-open spaces?

"You're being nice again," she said, a teasing lilt

to her voice. "While I appreciate it, I'm sure you have better things you could be doing tonight than this."

"Nope." He shook his head. "Driving down the highway with you tops my list." He made the comment casually, because he didn't exactly want to share how much this moment meant to him.

"If that's the case, I bet you're champing at the bit to get back to your regular life."

"I'm enjoying the break."

"Really?" She shifted in her seat to look at him more fully. "Tell me about Chicago. The city must be so exciting. I've always wanted to visit."

"The pace is definitely different than you have around here, but not necessarily better. Just different."

"What would you be doing on a normal weekday night if you were in the city?"

He glanced at the clock on the dashboard. "Most likely I'd still be at the office."

"Describe it," she said. "Did you decorate it yourself?"

He chuckled at her attention to detail. "Not really, although I worked with the firm's interior designer to choose paint colors and a few pieces of generic art. If my diploma weren't hanging on the wall, the space could belong to anyone."

"But you spend a lot of time there. Are you part of a big firm?"

He nodded and explained how he'd interviewed

with several law firms during his final semester at law school and chosen this one because of its size and the variety of clients. At the time, Wiley had been captivated by the thought of working in an office with a dozen other associates. He'd assumed he'd have the chance to work with myriad different types of clients, although in reality the work was more monotonous than varied.

As Grace peppered him with questions about his coworkers, his hobbies and his friends, he realized how one-dimensional he'd allowed his life to become. Much like a robot, he functioned on autopilot. Not that daily life in Rambling Rose was a roller coaster of excitement, but observing his siblings for the past week, he realized that they'd managed to create rich, layered lives filled with friends, new ventures and sometimes love.

He had very little to share that made his life sound fun. Hell, he'd even gotten into the habit of ordering the same rotation of meals from the carryout restaurant around the corner from his condo. He had all the freedom in the world, he realized, but took advantage of none of it.

As quickly as possible, he turned the conversation toward Grace's life. She recounted in more detail the aftermath of her brother's car accident and what it had meant for her. She didn't complain about having to leave college to help with Jake's recovery, and he admired her dedication to her family and her positive attitude.

He wanted to ask more about her time at the cowboy-themed amusement park his relatives ran in the small town of Horseback Hollow, but she suddenly sat forward in the seat. "Get off here," she told him, and he veered onto the exit ramp, although he hadn't even noticed a sign for services along the empty stretch of ranch land.

"We came here when I was a kid," she told him, looking around with a sentimental gleam in her eye.

"Where exactly is here?"

"Turn right off the exit." She pulled her phone from the purse she'd looped around her shoulder. "Shoot. I don't have service, but I'm pretty sure there's a restaurant about a mile down the road."

"In the middle of nowhere?" He grinned at her. "Should I be concerned about what they might be serving on the menu?"

"It's part of the adventure," she told him. "Let yourself go crazy, Counselor."

"So long as crazy doesn't end up with either of us hugging the porcelain throne later tonight."

She laughed at that, and the sound reverberated through him like music. He still couldn't tell what it was about Grace, but Wiley felt completely at ease with her.

The road wound in a gentle curve, grand oak trees flanking it. He liked the differences in the north

Texas landscape. The way the scenery could change from wide-open fields to rows of trees standing sentry, their bare branches reaching toward the heavens.

Suddenly, a small house—or inn—appeared in a clearing. The decades-old structure was painted deep purple with a yard filled with whirligigs and metal lawn art out front.

"That's it." Grace clasped her hands together. "I remember the sculptures. I was fascinated with watching them move when we came here."

He pulled into the gravel parking lot, which was half-filled with cars. "I can't believe you found this place," he said, grinning at the happiness in Grace's blue eyes. She looked like a kid about to enter her favorite candy store.

"I can't believe it, either." She reached out and squeezed his hand. "It must be a sign."

He lifted a brow. "Of what?"

"This is the moment my luck changes. No more cheating boyfriends or accidents or dead-end jobs. This place shows that I can find something great if I trust my instincts."

Wiley turned over his hand so their palms touched, once more amazed at how soft her skin felt against his. He wasn't certain he believed in luck or signs, but he knew enough to savor this moment and his time with Grace.

"Then let's go try your luck with the Oak Tree Inn."

By the time he pulled her crutches from the back seat and made his way around the car, Grace had climbed out, gazing at the inn's clapboard front like it was the entrance to Shangri-la.

She adjusted the crutches under her arm and started toward the building, stumbling slightly when the bottom of a crutch slipped on a large rock.

"I've got it," she said before he could offer assistance.

Her quiet independence was a new experience for Wiley. Although he kept his romantic life casual, he definitely had a type. Gorgeous, young and happy to have him take care of everything from planning dates to choosing menu items and definitely setting limits on how close he would get. He tended to go out with women whom his sisters liked to describe as damsels in distress. It wasn't as if he purposely sought out the role of "knight in shining Italian loafers" but that was often the position he found himself in.

He expected things to be the same with Grace, especially given what she'd been through. Her injuries were the perfect excuse to sit back and let him pamper her, which he would be happy to do.

But the more time he spent with her, the more he understood that making her own way was important to Grace. She didn't want to be handled or coddled, despite all the stumbling blocks life had put in her way. Her determination captivated him. Maybe that's why he found himself becoming more and more fascinated by her with every passing minute.

Grace couldn't remember a night when she'd had more fun than she had spending the evening with Wiley.

They sat near the firepit on the back deck of the cozy inn, the only two people who'd ventured out from the dining room. Dinner had been even yummier than she imagined, with the chef offering simple dishes with an Italian flair.

Her frustrations and struggles with work and her family seemed a million miles away. To her great relief, Wiley appeared just as relaxed as she felt. The inn's owner had given them a couple of thick fleece blankets to take out with them, and they sat close together on an outdoor love seat.

"This is how I want people to feel when they stay at the Hotel Fortune," she murmured, her breath catching as Wiley shifted so that their thighs pressed against each other.

"Blissed out on good food?" he asked with a wink.

"Happy," she answered simply.

Her response seemed to catch him off guard, and he gazed into the fire for several long seconds before speaking.

"I feel it, too." His voice was a quiet rumble and did funny things to Grace's insides. "Happy."

He bent forward to place his wineglass on the stamped concrete patio.

"But I think my happiness has more to do with you than this place." He gestured to the building behind him. "Or the food and drinks, although everything was fantastic."

Pleasure swirled through her at his words, because she felt the exact same way. Grace reminded herself that she not only didn't believe in love at first sight, but she wasn't interested in anything that would take her focus from her position at the hotel and the potential of earning the coveted general manager promotion.

"But if we can offer our guests—both local and out-of-town visitors—an experience that lets them forget the troubles of regular life so quickly, they'll definitely come back over and over."

Her lips tingled when he placed a gentle finger against them. "I thought we agreed no work talk tonight."

She gave a shaky nod, then wrapped her fingers around his. "Yes, but you know I'm right."

He chuckled. "You're right," he conceded without hesitation. "This night is special."

Then he leaned close and brushed his mouth over hers. It was a tentative kiss, a question of sorts. Grace couldn't tell which one of them he expected to answer. Her body had no doubt, however, and she reached up and wound her hands around his neck, needing to be close to him.

A low groan escaped Wiley's lips, and it felt like a gift that she could affect a man like him. He cupped her face between his big hands, angling her head and deepening the kiss. Their tongues met and melded, making heat shoot through Grace's body in a way that shocked and thrilled her. No simple kiss had ever stirred her in this way.

Normally, she would wait for a man to push for more, but Wiley seemed content to savor her and the moment like they had all the time in the world to discover each other. Within moments, Grace lost herself in the sensation.

After what felt like hours but was probably only minutes, Wiley pulled away. He stared into her eyes without speaking, but his gaze told her everything she needed to know. "Wow," he murmured, one side of his mouth curving.

"Exactly what I was thinking." She went to shift closer and banged her foot on the edge of the love seat, and muffled a yelp of pain. Nothing like the reminder of her injury to put a damper on the most romantic interlude she'd had in forever.

"Are you okay?" Wiley's hand immediately went to her leg, and Grace lost all ability to think coherently.

"Fine," she managed, trying not to wheeze. "But maybe you should kiss me again and make it better."

He flashed a wolfish grin and claimed her mouth again.

Grace jerked back when she heard the sound of voices headed in their direction. Two older couples were walking toward the firepit from the restaurant.

"We should probably go," Grace said, although she didn't want the moment to end. She didn't want anything about this night to end.

"Will your parents be worried?"

She shook her head. "I texted my mom while you were in the restroom so she doesn't worry. It's weird to be an adult and still check in, but she appreciates it." She stifled a yawn. "I wish I had my normal energy."

"You're overdoing it." Wiley immediately shrugged off the blanket, stood and then scooped her into his arms.

Grace sputtered out a shocked protest. "I'm not that tired."

"Could you hand me those crutches?" Wiley asked one of the men from the group that circled the other side of the firepit.

The stranger did as he was asked while the two women looked on with similar expressions of fascination. "That's so sweet," one of them told the other.

Color rushed to Grace's cheeks. "You can put me down," she said into Wiley's ear.

"Young love," the second woman responded. "If

Carl tried to pick me up like that, he'd pull out his back."

The women laughed as Wiley started down the back steps and around the side of the inn. They'd already paid their bill so didn't need to return inside.

"Wiley." Grace squeezed his shoulder. "You don't need to carry me."

He paused and kissed her again. "I know you're more than capable on your own, Grace. But please let me hold you for a few minutes."

Well, when he put it like that, how could she refuse?

Reassured that he wasn't taking pity on her, she settled into his embrace for the short walk to the parking lot. He was warm and strong, and she couldn't resist tracing one finger along the strong column of his neck. His Adam's apple bobbed as he swallowed.

"You're going to cause me to stumble, and we'll both hit the ground," he said with a gruff laugh.

"I trust you."

His arms tightened around her for a few blissful seconds, and then they were at the car. He deposited her on the ground and rested her crutches against the back door.

"Thank you," he said, and pressed a gentle kiss to her forehead.

"I think I should be thanking you." She grinned.

"As should those two women at the firepit. From the sound of it, you made their night with your heroics."

His gaze darkened. "I'm not a hero. I just wanted an excuse to wrap my arms around you."

"Do you need an excuse?"

He turned his head, as if he needed to look away in order to gather his thoughts. "I like you, Grace. A lot. From the moment I saw you at the birthday party, there was something…"

"I know," she said, lifting a hand to his jaw. "I felt the same thing."

He met her gaze once again. "I don't want to take advantage of you."

Please, her body screamed silently. *Take advantage*.

"I'm a big girl, Wiley."

"I'm only in town until the hotel's grand opening," he reminded her, as if she could forget.

"That gives us a few more weeks."

One side of his mouth twitched. "What exactly did you have in mind during that time?"

Heat pooled low in her belly, but there was no way she could articulate all the things she had in mind for Wiley. Her uninjured leg began to ache, an outward sign of her current limitations. The cast was going to make anything physical between them awkward at best.

Then she realized that as much as she desired the man standing in front of her, she liked talking to him and just being around him as much if not more. He made her feel smart and capable. Right now she wanted—needed—more of that in her life.

"We could hang out," she suggested. "Like tonight."

"Tonight was a date."

The words sent pleasure spiraling through her. "Then we could date more."

His thick brows drew together. "Until the opening?"

She nodded. "You're returning to Chicago, and I'm focused on my career. Neither of us has time for anything serious, but we have fun together. Right?"

"So much fun," he murmured, still teasing.

"It's a mutually beneficial arrangement." Grace held her breath as she waited for his response. In truth she barely recognized herself, suggesting a short-term fling with a man like Wiley. The brother of her bosses at the hotel.

There were so many reasons it might be a bad idea, not the least of which was the way he made her heart stutter and her body ache when he looked at her. And when he kissed her...

She couldn't focus on the risks. Grace had spent so long playing it safe. Her vow when she'd returned to Rambling Rose had been to live life to the fullest, to push herself out of her comfort zone. This was definitely ticking off those boxes.

Wiley's dark gaze searched her face for several

FREE BOOKS GIVEAWAY

2 FREE
ROMANCE
BOOKS!

2 FREE
WHOLESOME
ROMANCE
BOOKS!

GET UP TO FOUR FREE BOOKS
& TWO FREE GIFTS
WORTH OVER $20!

We pay for everything!

Dear Reader,

I am writing to announce the launch of a huge **FREE BOOK GIVEAWAY**... and to let you know that YOU are entitled to choose up to FOUR fantastic books that WE pay for.

Try **Harlequin® Special Edition** books featuring comfort and strength in the support of loved ones and enjoying the journey no mader what life throws your way.

Try **Harlequin® Heartwarming™ Larger-Print** books featuring uplifting stories where the bonds of friendship, family and community unite.

Or TRY BOTH!

In return, we ask just one favor: Would you please participate in our brief Reader Survey? We'd love to hear from you.

This FREE BOOK GIVEAWAY means that we pay for *everything!* We'll even cover the shipping, and no purchase is necessary, now or later. So please return your survey today. You'll get **Two Free Books** and **Two Mystery Gifts** from each series to try, altogether worth over **$20!**

Sincerely

Pam Powers

Pam Powers
For Harlequin Reader Service

Complete the survey below and return
it today to receive up to 4 FREE BOOKS
and FREE GIFTS guaranteed!

HARLEQUIN READER SERVICE—Here's how it works:

seconds, and then he nodded. "This is the start of a few weeks of as much mutually beneficial fun as we can manage."

Chapter Eight

Wiley followed the sound of construction toward the hotel's back patio two days later. He'd spent most of the previous day holed up in his bedroom suite at the ranch, on a never-ending stream of calls and videoconferences. Working remotely was turning out to be more of a challenge than he'd expected, but the thought of returning to Chicago held little appeal, especially when staying in Texas meant spending time with Grace.

He'd walked her to her parents' front door after their dinner together, and the urge to kiss her again had been difficult to resist. At least until her father opened the door as they climbed the porch steps, giving Wiley a look that clearly communicated Mike's disapproval.

After taking the crutches from him with a sigh, Grace had balanced herself on her uninjured leg and leaned in for a quick peck on his cheek and a murmured thank-you before disappearing into the house.

Her father had slammed the door in Wiley's face before he'd even had a chance to say goodbye. He'd climbed in his car and started toward home, pressing two fingers to the place her lips had touched, feeling like a lovesick teenager for wanting to vow not to wash that side of his face again.

Although Grace's mother seemed to approve of their friendship, it bothered Wiley that her dad and brother clearly wanted no part of him in Grace's life. He didn't date seriously, but Wiley had met his share of parents over the years, and all of them seemed inclined to support their daughters getting serious with an attorney, especially one who came from a well-to-do family. Wiley's stepfather, David, had made a fortune in the video game industry. He and his siblings were intent on carving their own path, yet there was no doubt in anyone's mind that they came from a good family.

Wiley would have thought the Fortune name garnered extra approval in Texas, where the expanded family had such a long and illustrious history. He knew better than to take Mike's and Jake's animosity personally. The idea that someone might have sabotaged the balcony's structural beams worried him, especially given what could have happened to Grace in the fall. But he was determined to prove that he only had Grace's best interests in mind.

Callum waved to him as he stepped out into the bright sunlight of the mid-January day. Wiley glanced at the workers on ladders affixing new lumber to the hotel's exterior. Once local law enforcement and the insurance company finished their investigations, the crew had wasted no time in cleaning up the fallen balcony and starting to rebuild.

"You're making great progress," he said as he joined Callum.

His brother gave a tight nod. "We need to have the balcony reconstructed completely before the opening. I want this place to look like an accident never happened."

Wiley drew in a deep breath. Callum was right, of course. It wouldn't do them any good for the hotel's reputation to be tainted even before they had their first paying guest. Hell, that was the whole point of the event Grace was coordinating. But it bothered him that they had no idea what or who had caused the problems with the beams. Their insurance company and the police might suspect sabotage, but they couldn't prove it.

Plans for the opening were moving ahead despite the shadow of potential foul play hanging over them. The fact that Kane had already begun the process of upgrading the property's security system gave Wiley a measure of comfort. Kane was also recommending that they take increased precautions at the other businesses in town, although no one wanted to believe the balcony collapse had been personal.

"I'm not saying I want to ignore what happened to Grace," Callum said, hands on his hips. "The safety of our employees and potential guests is the first priority."

"I know," Wiley agreed. "But I don't like loose ends. If we knew for certain what had caused the accident—either way—I'd feel better."

"I feel the same, but we can't let that derail us from our goal."

They both turned as a feminine voice called a greeting. Mariana approached from the far side of the pool, her bleached blond hair pulled into a loose ponytail and reading glasses resting on top of her head. Her smile faltered slightly as she glanced up to the second floor, but it was bright once more when she returned her gaze to the brothers.

"Good morning, Fortunes," she said, holding up several brown paper bags. "I've brought lunch for your crew."

There was a resounding cheer from the men, who'd all turned to watch Mariana. The woman truly was a force of nature and well-loved in the Rambling Rose community.

"That's the best thing I've heard all day," Callum

said, returning her grin as he took one of the bags. "To what do we owe the pleasure?"

She placed a bejeweled hand on his shoulder. "Ah, Callum. I'm here spreading sunshine and light in the form of my famous empanadas."

Wiley chuckled. "Food that makes everything better. That could be your new tagline." And he had no doubt it was true. Mariana had run her popular food truck for years at Mariana's Marketplace, Rambling Rose's busy flea market. Last year, she took an active role in the town's future businesses and even discovered a connection to the Fortunes through the town's old Foundling Hospital.

His brothers and sisters had been wise to involve Mariana in the hotel's development. She helped Nicole run the Roja kitchen and brought her usual enthusiasm and style to that role. Everyone on staff seemed to love her, and Wiley felt like she might give additional credibility to the venture. Not many people in town would go up against the formidable Mariana.

"How is Grace Williams?" she asked Callum.

Wiley forced himself not to answer, although his brother sent him a curious look. On the way home from dinner, Grace had told him she wanted to keep anything other than friendship strictly between them. He rubbed the heel of his hand against his chest to ease the ache that suddenly appeared there. It made no sense that he felt disappointed at the thought of not being able to publicly claim Grace as his, even temporarily.

He understood the rationale, given her position in the training program and the impending announcement about the general manager promotion. Although he would never try to influence his brothers or sisters based on his personal feelings, there was no need to in this case. After spending more time with the other trainees, particularly Jillian Steward, Wiley felt even more certain that Grace should earn the new role. Jillian rubbed him the wrong way, always trying to make it seem like she was in charge. He liked one of the other trainees, an easygoing man named Jay Cross, well enough, but Jay seemed more interested in filling in wherever needed than adept at running the entire hotel.

"From what she tells us, she's doing better." Callum nodded. "The event she's putting together is going to be a huge success. We had a phone meeting yesterday, and she's gotten the whole thing coordinated in less than a week."

"She was always such a hard worker," Mariana murmured thoughtfully. "I hope she's not overdoing it."

"Me, too."

Wiley could feel Callum's gaze on him but ignored it.

"She did look a little worn down on the call," Callum continued, turning to Mariana.

Wiley sucked in a breath. Worn down? He hadn't seen Grace since their date, but they'd been texting regularly, and he was supposed to pick her up for dinner after work tonight.

"The accident could have been so much worse," Mariana said. "She needs to make rest a priority."

Callum nodded. "Agreed, although it's hard to convince her of that. I'm going to ask Nicole or Megan to reach out, as well. We scheduled a physical therapist to work with her on any lingering soreness or potential back issues. The ankle is the most obvious injury, but she mentioned the doctor was worried about mobility and her range of motion."

"She told you that?" Wiley ran a hand through his hair and tried to mask his reaction. Grace hadn't talked to him about other injuries.

"Yeah," his brother answered. "But she hasn't returned the PT's calls. Knowing Grace, she feels like she's taking advantage since she knows we're paying for it."

"The money doesn't matter," Wiley said, realizing the harshness of his tone when both Callum and Mariana startled.

"I understand," Callum told him. "We all do. Someone just needs to convince Grace of that. I'm sure one of the triplets can—"

"I'll handle it," Wiley said.

Mariana shook her head. "Grace has always been determined to make her own way. She'd probably respond better to one of your sisters since she knows them."

"She knows me," Wiley said, making his voice gentle. "We're friends."

"Friends?" Mariana murmured while Callum shook his head.

"You don't have friends," his brother said. "You have us, coworkers and the arm candy you date."

"Wow. That's a real shot in the arm. Trust me. Grace and I are friends, and I'll convince her to work with the physical therapist." He looked between the two of them. "For the record, she's not the delicate flower that everyone around here assumes her to be. She's strong and capable, and it's about time people stop underestimating her."

When both Callum and Mariana appeared to be shocked into silence, Wiley turned and stalked away.

"You saw Wiley a couple of nights ago. I thought we were going to hang out tonight."

Grace paused in the act of applying mascara and looked at her brother in the mirror that hung above the dresser in her childhood bedroom. It still amazed her that their parents hadn't changed either her bedroom or Jake's since they'd moved out. She vaguely remembered that her mother had been planning on a whole house clean-out just before Jake's accident. Everything had been put on hold in the months after that as they all rallied around him to support his recovery.

"I know you have something better to do than watch movies with your little sister." She pointed the mascara wand at Jake. "I heard you were becoming pretty chummy with Melissa Wagner."

Jake made a face. "Shouldn't you be busy resting and getting better? Why do you have time for petty gossip about my love life?"

"Because I've been doing very little other than resting." She placed the mascara tube on the glass charger that held her simple supply of cosmetics and turned. "I need to get out more."

"That's not true." Jake adjusted the pillow he'd propped behind his head as he sprawled across her comforter. "Mom and Dad are already worried about how much time you're devoting to this hotel event, and it's not good for anyone—especially you—to be spending time with some big-city attorney."

"We're friends." Grace hopped over to the closet to pull out a jacket, not wanting her brother to witness the heat she could feel crawling up her cheeks at the thought of Wiley. They'd agreed to keep their relationship secret, so she couldn't give her feelings away to her brother. Feelings that were probably not wise, given that Wiley was leaving town after the grand opening.

She might have suggested a short-term arrangement with her mind dizzy from his kisses, but in the past couple days she'd realized that wouldn't stop her heart from wanting more.

Jake gestured to the arrangement of flowers that sat on the taller dresser. "Why does a friend send you flowers? And cheesecake?" He snorted. "Who sends a woman cheesecake?"

"Um...you better not complain after I saw you scarf down a huge slice when Mom told you about it."

"Well, I love cheesecake."

"Me, too." Grace pulled on her jacket. "I happened to mention it to Wiley, and he told me about some bakery in New York City that makes the best."

"And then had it sent to you? Classic rich-boy move."

"Don't be a jerk, Jake. This whole business with the accident has been hard. I hate having people look at me with pity or reminding me that I'm lucky to be alive."

"Trust me, I get that."

She heard the bitterness in her brother's tone and immediately regretted her comment. "I know you do. So I hope you can also understand that I like Wiley. He's nice, and he doesn't treat me like I'm weak. He helps take my mind off of what happened."

"I get it." Jake sat up straighter with a sigh. "But that's what I'm worried about, Gracie. I don't trust the Fortunes, and especially not the attorney. Don't you think it's a little too convenient that he just happened to decide to stay in Rambling Rose after the balcony collapsed?"

"He wants to make sure everything goes smoothly with plans for the opening. He's supporting his family." She drew in a deep breath and added, "He's supporting me."

Jake studied her for several moments, and Grace decided she wasn't going to hide her emotions from her brother. She was a grown woman and could make her own choices about who she spent her time with.

"Don't let him take advantage of you," he warned, his gentle tone almost harder to handle than the snarky remarks he'd made earlier.

"I trust him," she said, because that was the only truth that mattered to her at the moment.

The sound of the doorbell had her turning for the hallway. "Come back tomorrow night, Jake. I'll kick your butt in Scrabble."

"You wish." He climbed off her bed and followed her out of the room. "I don't suppose you want me to greet the Fortune with you?"

"Can you be nice?" she asked over her shoulder.

He pounded a fist to his chest like she'd wounded him. "Of course I can. I just prefer not to."

She smiled despite her annoyance and made her way down the hall. Once again, she'd left her crutches in the front entry. Although she didn't enjoy hopping around her parents' house, the hallway was narrow, and the rooms were filled with furniture that made it difficult to maneuver with crutches.

Her parents were in the backyard discussing plans for a garden bed her mom wanted in the spring. She desperately needed to get to the door and away from the house before they realized Wiley had arrived to pick her up. She knew her mom would be nice but couldn't say the same for her dad. He was almost as bad as Jake as far as doubting Wiley's motives. She could only imagine what they would think if they knew she was dating the handsome Fortune.

She opened the door and smiled at him, anticipation curling in her belly as she waited for his greeting.

"Hello, Grace," he said in that smooth tone, and she felt her grin widen. Did he even realize what those two words did to her?

"Hi." She groaned in frustration when one of the crutches slipped from her hand and clattered to the floor. "I swear I'm going to get better with these before I get to the hotel."

Wiley bent and retrieved the crutch, handing it to her. "I have a better idea." He reached to one side of the door and pulled a black scooter into view. It had foam handles and a wide pad clearly meant for her injured leg. "I brought you a gift."

Grace's mouth dropped open. "Oh, my gosh. My own set of wheels?"

Wiley nodded. "I called a doctor friend, and he

suggested it. Apparently, it's a lot easier to maneuver and can help with your mobility. Not that you aren't doing great with the crutches."

"I hate the crutches." She put her hands on the scooter's handle and then lifted her leg onto the long black cushion. It was so easy to push herself to the far side of the porch and then turn the scooter to head back toward Wiley. "I'm a natural on this."

When she got close to the door, she called for her brother. It didn't matter what Jake thought about Wiley. He had to see her scooter.

He appeared in the doorway a moment later. "Wow. That's cool, Gracie. Where'd you get the spankin' new ride?"

"Wiley brought it for me. It's amazing, right?"

"Yeah." Jake crossed his muscled arms over his chest as he glanced at Wiley. "Nice work, Fortune."

"Thanks," Wiley muttered.

Grace laughed at the two men, who looked equally uncomfortable exchanging even the most basic pleasantries.

"Tell Mom and Dad not to wait up," she said to her brother. "Now that I actually get around, who knows what fun we can find."

"It's Rambling Rose," Jake said with a wry laugh. "We all know there are limits to the fun you can have in this town."

"I don't know about that." Wiley lifted the scooter when Grace took hold of the staircase railing.

Grace was glad she had her back to her brother, because she couldn't prevent the wide grin at the thought of all the fun she and Wiley could have together.

Chapter Nine

"I'm not sure this is such a good idea." Grace leaned forward to look at the entrance of Provisions, the farm-to-table restaurant Wiley's sisters ran in town, along with Ashley's fiancé, Rodrigo Mendoza. "I thought we agreed to keep our relationship between us."

"We're friends," Wiley assured her. "Everyone in my family likes you, and they don't need to know more than I'm helping you out with a ride. I haven't had a chance to do more than stop by the restaurant. Ashley won't quit giving me grief." He flashed what he hoped amounted to a convincing smile. "You'd be doing me a huge favor."

"I guess," she relented after a few seconds of chewing on her bottom lip. "I've wanted to eat here since they opened Provisions last year. Plus, I need to be familiar with other restaurants in town so I can make recommendations to hotel guests. Right?"

"Exactly. This is a perfect excuse for that. But if you aren't comfortable with it, we can drive out of town and—"

"Let's eat here." She reached out and squeezed his arm. "But no kissing."

He chuckled. "That's a bummer. Can we find some place to park after dinner so we can make out in my car like a couple of teenagers?"

"You joke, but I'm serious. I don't want anyone in your family to know we're dating."

"Our secret is safe with me." Wiley kept his smile on his face as he climbed out the car, ignoring the pang of disappointment that stabbed his gut knowing that Grace wanted to keep what was between them hidden. Her insistence on secrecy was an unwelcome reminder that their relationship was temporary. Of course, he knew it. After all, he'd be returning to Chicago in a matter of weeks, and Grace would be busy with the hotel. He should be feeling relief. Normally, he was the one placing parameters on his dating life about what he was and wasn't willing to offer. A few weeks was plenty of time to get a woman out of his system, but somehow Wiley knew Grace wasn't like other women.

He thought back to that moment he'd spotted her across the Roja banquet room and the word that had whispered inside him like trace of a melody he couldn't quite place. *Mine*. The idea was ridiculous, and he knew it. Grace didn't belong to anyone but herself. That didn't stop Wiley from wanting her. From wanting more.

As he retrieved the scooter from the trunk, he tried to shake off his disturbing train of thought. Obviously, he was just reacting to being away from his regular life. He didn't have his work and his hectic schedule to keep him busy, so he had too much time to think about Grace. Once he returned to Chicago, things would get back to normal. No way was he falling under the spell of this sleepy Texas town the way his siblings had.

Grace was already standing next to the car, using the open passenger door for balance, when he got there.

She smiled up at him, a teasing light in her eyes. "You might have all the willpower, but it's going to be hard for me not to kiss you."

Just like that, every last one of Wiley's rationales about remaining distant or getting her out of his system disappeared like a puff of smoke in a brisk wind.

"Later," he promised, brushing his hand against hers. "Save that thought for later."

"Who was the first girl you kissed?" Grace asked

as they made their way toward the restaurant's entrance.

"Jessica Meyer in seventh grade. We were in the same math class, and she was way smarter than me."

"You were a late bloomer," Grace said, clearly delighted. "I kissed Miles Spicaro on the playground in second grade."

"Not Collin?" Wiley asked, then regretted the question. He felt like a fool revealing how much her friendship with the boy—now man—next door bothered him.

She gave him a funny look. "Not Collin. And Miles ended up being a onetime interlude. Too much pressure for elementary school. What about this Jessica? Was it first love?"

Wiley opened the heavy wood door to Provisions and gestured Grace forward. "I've never had a first love."

"Oh." That one syllable conveyed so much about what she thought of his confession, and once more, he wished he would have kept his personal business to himself. It wasn't like him to share details about his feelings or really anything with the women he dated. He hadn't planned on not falling in love, of course. He wasn't completely coldhearted.

But love meant compromise, and Wiley valued his independence too much to give it up on any meaningful level. At least that's what he told himself.

"Hi, guys." Ashley met them at the hostess stand

when they entered the restaurant. She gave Grace a one-armed hug and touched a finger to the scab that had almost completely healed on Grace's forehead. "You look amazing, and I love that scooter. How are you feeling?"

"Thank you," Grace answered almost shyly. "I'm doing better every day and looking forward to getting back to work. Wiley found the scooter, and it's a huge improvement over the crutches. I could never quite find my balance with them."

"Nice work, Wi." Ashley turned to hug him. "Did you just eat a lemon?"

He frowned at the question. "No, why?"

"Your face is all puckered. Is something wrong?"

He shook his head, willing some random alien ship to appear and beam his sister up into its depths. Grace was looking at him oddly now that Ashley had pointed out his lemon face. Even though he was certain he didn't have any kind of furrowed expression. He simply didn't want to think about what he couldn't give to a woman like Grace.

"Everything is great. We're excited for dinner." He gestured to the dining room. "You have quite a crowd."

Ashley followed his gaze to the open-concept restaurant, situated with tables filled with customers. "I hope the hotel does as well as we are. It's beyond my wildest dreams."

"We're going to make sure the hotel is a huge success," Grace offered. "Your brothers and sisters have been working so hard to get things ready."

"With your help," Ashley answered. "From what Nicole says, they miss having you at work. Not that the other trainees aren't doing a great job, but…"

Grace nodded, color blooming on her cheeks. "I can't wait to be back."

"You all need to stop pressuring her," Wiley grumbled, hating that he sounded like some kind of overprotective grandpa. But he couldn't stop himself. After speaking to Callum and Mariana about Grace not following up on the PT appointments, he wondered if anxiety about returning to work was making her sacrifice her recovery.

Were her parents actually right?

"No pressure," Ashley promised as she led them through the dining room. "You getting well is the top priority."

"I'm really feeling much better," Grace assured her, darting a quelling glance at Wiley over her shoulder.

Ashley opened the door to a private room on one side of the restaurant. "I hope it's okay with both of you, but we prepared a special tasting menu for to-night." She grinned at Wiley. "I want a chance to im-press my big brother and figured you might enjoy a bit of privacy." She gave Grace a sympathetic nod. "It feels like everyone is still talking about the ac-cident, you know?"

"I do," Grace agreed with a grateful smile. "I hate being a topic of conversation. Thank you for your thoughtfulness, Ashley. I really appreciate it."

As his sister closed the door to the private dining area, Wiley glanced around the space, pleased at how things had turned out. He'd suggested to Ashley that Grace didn't like the attention she was receiving for her injury, feeling like that was a plausible reason to request a space of their own.

The room retained the character of the grain silo that had once occupied the space, with high ceilings and painted shiplap on the walls. A white cloth covered an impeccably set table in the middle of the room. Grace wheeled the scooter slowly toward the table, taking in the flowers and candles on the sideboard. He wondered what would happen if he told her how he was truly coming to feel about her—the way his heart stammered every time he looked at her and the anticipation of seeing one of her sweet smiles. Would she admit to the same level of connection, or would he scare her away by deviating from the path they'd agreed to?

Was he brave enough to risk finding out?

Just as he was about to speak, she turned to him, and the anger flashing in her blue eyes took him by surprise.

"Do you think I need to be coddled in the same way my parents do?" she whispered, the pain in her voice cutting off all thoughts of a revelation about his feelings. Confusion filled him, and he wanted a do-over on the past few minutes. Apparently, Wiley had misjudged her reaction to his plan for a private dinner in a monumental way.

Grace regretted the words as soon as they left her mouth. She looked away from Wiley's shocked expression and took in the beauty of the room. From the soft lighting punctuated with flickering candles to the scent of flowers perfuming the air, she couldn't have asked for a more romantic setup. Calla lilies took center stage in the flower arrangements, not a surprise since Wiley knew they were her favorite.

She had no doubt he'd orchestrated this room and the mood it set. She didn't want to consider what the attention to detail that had gone into it might reveal to the Provisions staff—and more importantly to his sister—about the nature of their relationship. She'd expect nothing less of her big-city attorney. From food to the little gifts and flowers he'd brought her, it was clear he was a master of thoughtful gestures.

As much as she appreciated being spoiled in this way, what Grace liked best about Wiley was that he'd seemed to believe in her. He hadn't treated her like a child the way her parents tended to. Despite her struggles, he never gave any indication that he thought her incapable of dealing with challenges or making her own decisions.

Until tonight.

"I don't know what you're talking about." He shook his head. "I'm not trying to coddle you, Grace."

"Then why mention to your sister how I need to make recovering my priority as if I'm not already doing that?" She moved closer to the table. "You sound like my dad or Jake. I thought you believed I could manage my own life?"

"I do."

"That's not what it sounded like." She dashed a hand across her cheek, cursing the tears that gathered in her eyes. She didn't want to cry but was working so hard to prove that she could handle everything. The truth was, sometimes she doubted herself. She felt tired and achy and like she wanted to crawl into bed, but she kept going. She wouldn't have the opportunity for the promotion at the hotel taken from her because she wasn't up to the task of it.

"Grace." He stepped closer, and she wanted to back away, but that wasn't so easy to manage with the scooter. "I know how determined you are to return to the hotel, even though you're practically managing as much as two people working remotely. But I'd be lying if I told you I wasn't worried about you."

Betrayal ripped through her, but he held up a hand before she could speak. "Tell me why you haven't contacted the physical therapist my family arranged."

"How do you know about that?" she demanded instead of answering, hating to be put on the spot in this way.

"Callum mentioned it," he said gently. "You understand that people realize how serious the fall could have been? More serious than it was." He paused, looked away for moment before his gaze returned to hers. "Deadly."

"Of course I do." She squeezed her eyes shut. "And I hate it. I hate that people are talking about me or feeling sorry for me." She slapped her hand against the scooter's metal frame. "I hate that the cast is a visible reminder of the accident. I'm forever going to be associated with this black spot that I'm sure everyone at the Hotel Fortune would like to erase."

"They don't want to erase you, sweetheart." He took her hand and lifted it to his lips, placing a kiss on each one of her knuckles.

"No kissing," she reminded him, but didn't pull away.

"You're too hard to resist." He inclined his head. "Will you make an appointment with the PT? I know how strong you are. And brave. I know that you'll work through almost anything, but that doesn't mean I don't worry." He leaned in, his forehead pressing against hers in a way that felt strangely intimate. "Not like your parents, Grace. I worry like a man who cares about a woman. The fact that I want you to take care of yourself doesn't mean I don't believe in you."

"Okay," she answered, unsure that her jumbled

brain was capable of saying anything more. He cared about her. What did that mean?

Because she knew what it meant for her. It meant that her heart was happy when Wiley was around and that the depth of feeling she already had for him scared her to her core. She knew what it was like to have her heart broken, and here she was risking it with a man who'd just blithely told her he'd never been in love.

It wasn't as if she thought he was going to change for her, despite how much she might want him to try.

Yet she had to admit he was right about pushing herself. "I don't want the Fortunes to think I'm trying to take advantage of them or that I think they're responsible for me being hurt. It felt like if I worked with a physical therapist on the injuries I have unrelated to my ankle, I'd be admitting that I was hurt more seriously than people thought." She placed a finger to his lips when he would have spoken. "Which I'm not, although my back is stiff, and I probably rely on over-the-counter anti-inflammatories more often than I should."

Wiley gave a sharp shake of his head. "That's it. I'm making sure the therapist is at your house first thing Monday morning."

Grace smiled. "I'm coming into the hotel next week for a meeting about the preopening event."

"No."

She rolled her eyes at him. "Wiley."

"Grace, you just admitted you're in pain. I hate the thought of you in pain."

She leaned in and kissed him, unable to stop herself. "I appreciate that and the fact that you're concerned and not overprotective. I'll call the PT and schedule a session for Monday afternoon, but no more talk about my injuries, especially with your siblings."

He looked like he wanted to argue, so she kissed him again.

"You can't resist me, either," he said with a sexy smirk as she pulled back.

"I guess you're right." Her heart hammered in her chest at the thought of how much she was already coming to care for him. A part of her wanted to tell him, but she was too afraid of scaring him off. Instead, she moved aside the scooter and eased herself into the chair. "Let's leave talk of the hotel behind tonight. I want to enjoy every moment of this friendly dinner."

To her great relief, he nodded and sat next to her. A discreet knock sounded on the door, and the server entered, carrying a tray filled with an assortment of appetizers that both smelled and looked divine.

Yes, Grace liked Wiley for the man he'd shown himself to be and the way he made her feel. She also appreciated that he wanted what was best for her, and tonight she was content to let herself be treated like someone special. She couldn't deny that she wanted more from him. Tomorrow she'd remind herself that her priority was proving herself at the hotel and winning the promotion. Tonight she'd let her heart lead the way.

Chapter Ten

"Are you sure you don't want me to help you in?" her mother asked as they rounded the corner toward the Hotel Fortune.

Grace blew out a huff of nervous laughter. "Mom, this isn't the first day of kindergarten."

"I get it," Barbara said with a chuckle. "I know you're a capable adult, Gracie. Your father and I are proud of how you've dealt with everything life has thrown your way. A lesser woman would have let it ruin them."

"I learned my strength from you," Grace said quietly.

It was true. After Jake's car accident, her mother

had never wavered in her outward confidence that her son would fully recover, despite the grueling process and all the setbacks they faced. Grace wanted to find a way to have that kind of faith in herself.

Her mother pulled to a stop at the curb in front of the hotel's main entrance. Grace smiled as she saw Jay Cross heading toward her.

"I've got this," Grace said as she opened her door, not sure who she was trying to convince.

"I love you, sweetie," Barbara said as she pushed the button to open the sedan's trunk. "I'd tell you to break a leg, but I'm afraid you might take me literally."

Grace turned to her mother with a smile. "I'll text you in a bit to let you know I'm fine."

A look of obvious relief crossed her mom's face, but she shook her head. "You don't have to, but I'd appreciate the update."

Jay had the scooter out of the trunk when Grace climbed out of the car. "Look at you, Ms. Overachiever," he said in his country drawl as she placed her purse and files in the scooter's wire basket and positioned her cast on the pad. "Are you trying to make the rest of us look like slackers?"

Excitement flooded through her as she looked at the hotel's stucco exterior. She tipped her head to the sky and said a silent thank-you for the ability to return to work and the beautiful day for it. "I'm a twenty-eight-year-old woman getting dropped off at

work by my mom." She lifted a brow. "She even offered to pack lunch for me, which is sweet but also
humiliating in a humbling way."

"I'll take your mom's lunch," Jay answered with
a laugh, running a hand through his cropped hair.

"You'll take free food from anyone." Grace started
for the hotel. "And we both know you aren't a slacker.
You're just strangely tranquil."

Jay looked startled for a brief moment before his
features shifted back to self-possessed. He was her
favorite person in the trainee program. His easygoing
attitude and willingness to pitch in made everything
more fun. He definitely cared about the hotel and he
worked hard, but didn't seem to have the same drive
as Jillian and Grace.

"Someone needs to be tranquil with Jillian taking
the lead in your absence."

Grace let out a small groan. "I was afraid of that."

"I don't think anyone is buying her 'I'm the second coming of Conrad Hilton' routine," Jay confided.
"But that isn't stopping her from trying to convince
them. It's like she's on a mission to suck up to every
Fortune in this town."

His derision was clear, and Grace appreciated that
he felt the same as she did about Jillian's attempts to
cast herself in the starring role for the hotel. But she
wondered if the Fortunes saw it that way.

Jillian had positive qualities. She was organized
and detail-oriented, but Grace had worked in hospi-

tality long enough to know that Jillian's snobby attitude would be a turnoff to certain guests. One of the cardinal rules about the hospitality industry was a focus on service, and in Grace's opinion, her rival still had a ways to go in learning to put the guests above her own ambition.

"I'm back," Grace murmured, unsure whether she was trying to reassure Jay or herself. "At least for a few hours every morning."

"How are you really feeling?" Jay asked, and she appreciated the concern in his voice.

"Other than the cast, I'm doing okay." She didn't bother mentioning the aches and pains she still had every morning. True to her word to Callum, she'd left a message for the physical therapist. She hadn't expected to hear back until today, but the woman had returned her call almost immediately. So fast, in fact, that Grace wondered if the PT had been instructed to respond as soon as Grace reached out. Either way, she was coming to the house for an initial consultation that afternoon. Although she'd been assured the hotel's insurance would cover all of the expenses related to her accident, Grace still didn't feel comfortable letting the Fortunes pay for the sessions, but she'd work that part out later.

Jay opened one of the hotel's large iron doors. She wheeled through and then gasped at the crowd of her coworkers congregating in front of the reservation desk. Everyone clapped for her arrival and several people—Nicole and Ashley included—held up signs welcoming her back.

Tears sprang to Grace's eyes, and she quickly tried to blink them away. Callum stood at the back of the crowd. He gave a slow nod as their gazes met. She'd wondered if anyone would even notice her absence, but this reception made her feel like the people at the hotel were truly a part of her family.

"I wasn't the only one who missed you," Jay said as he came to stand next to her.

"Welcome back, Grace." Callum stepped forward. "It's great to have you here again."

"Thank you," Grace answered, swallowing around the emotion clogging her throat. "A lot of people would be happy for an excuse to spend a few weeks binge-watching television, but it's a testament to all of you and how amazing this hotel is going to be that I just can't stay away. The Hotel Fortune will be the crowning jewel of this town, and I'm grateful to be even a small part of our success."

Another round of applause greeted her words, and Callum's grin broadened. He was such a serious man, focused and driven, so Grace felt particularly grateful that he seemed satisfied with her impromptu speech.

"We're the ones who are grateful to you," he told her, and then stepped aside so that other employees could greet her. It was almost fifteen minutes later before Grace was alone in the lobby with just Jillian and Jay. She stifled a yawn, wondering if her mom had been right and she was taking on too much.

How could talking make her so tired? She blamed it on the emotions of the morning, from returning to the hotel to the warm welcome she received and then being asked to recount the accident for her curious coworkers.

"You're like the mayor of this hotel," Jay said with a laugh as she turned to him and Jillian.

That comment earned a scowl from Jillian. "We have a meeting with Nicole to discuss restaurant logistics for the grand opening." She eyed Grace's leg. "I'm sure it will take a while for you to get up to speed. So much has happened since you've been on vacation."

"I wouldn't call it a vacation," Grace said, forcing her tone to remain steady.

Jillian waved a hand in front of her face. "Whatever. You practically just admitted that you've been doing nothing but watching television."

"And planning the preopening event," Jay added quietly.

"Busywork," Jillian muttered.

Grace smiled. Kill them with kindness, she thought. "I appreciate the two of you taking care of things while I was recovering. If there's anything you need me to pitch in on now that I'm back—"

"Part-time." Jillian sniffed. "No, I've got it handled. In fact, our meeting with Nicole is about to start." She gave Grace a condescending smile. "I scheduled us to meet in the banquet room upstairs. You probably don't want to deal with all those steps. They're doing maintenance on the elevators today, so they aren't an option."

Grace's heart sank as she glanced over to the bank of windows that overlooked the lobby from Roja's private room. The staircase was just off the entrance to the restaurant and would indeed be difficult for her to manage.

"How about if we switch the meeting to the first floor?" Jay glanced between the two women.

"There are things we need to discuss about seating arrangements upstairs," Jillian insisted. "Grace can check the hotel's email inbox while we're doing the important stuff. Of course, every little detail is important. You know what I mean."

Grace resisted the urge to grit her teeth. As difficult as she sometimes found it to stick up for herself, she had to start acting like a manager if that's what she wanted to be. "Jillian, I want to be part of the meeting. I'm sure Nicole will understand if we change the location."

At that moment, Nicole appeared at the Roja entrance situated off the lobby. She punched something into her cell phone, then shoved it into the back pocket of the stylish trousers she wore. "Did I hear you talking about a venue change?" she asked the three of them.

"Yes." Grace spoke before Jillian had a chance to. "Would it be okay if we met down here so that I don't have to contend with the stairs? I have some ideas I think you'll want to hear."

"Great idea," Nicole said easily. "I want everyone to contribute."

Jillian's face went blank. "But we have seating charts to discuss so we should be upstairs if—"

"We'll manage. We can review the charts on the digital floor plan." Nicole gave a pointed look to the tablet Jillian carried. "Grace, I can't wait to hear your thoughts on plans for the grand opening. You've done such an amazing job so far with the pre-event."

"Thanks," Grace whispered. Clearly annoyed and just as clearly trying to hide it, Jillian followed Nicole into the restaurant. Jay held open the door for Grace, who wheeled forward, proud of her tiny victory in derailing Jillian's attempt at undermining her. Grace was no longer going to fade into the background for anyone.

"Thank you for the ride," Grace said later that afternoon as Wiley pulled out of the hotel's parking lot. "My mom or Jake could have picked me up."

"It's not a problem," he told her. "I'm heading back to the Fame and Fortune anyway to work on some contracts that came in for review earlier."

She rolled her head on the seat back to look at him. "It must be difficult to balance everything you've taken on at the hotel with the work from your regular job."

He shrugged. "I don't mind."

"Because it's temporary?" She couldn't help but ask, needing the reminder not to get used to Wiley's presence in her life, no matter how much she wanted to.

"Because I like the work I do at the law firm, and I enjoy helping my family."

His magnanimous answer made her feel petty and small. There was no reason to goad Wiley, especially when he'd been so kind and helpful.

"That's nice," she said when her exhausted brain couldn't come up with anything better.

"Are you okay?" He reached across the console and placed a warm hand on the top of her thigh. "Did you have a good morning at the hotel?"

She nodded. "Yes. I liked feeling productive, and it was so nice of everyone on staff to welcome me back." She stifled a yawn. "But it makes me mad to get so tired after only working a few hours. I'm used to being able to go all day and still have energy left over. Now I feel like I just ran a marathon."

"It will get better. Your body is still healing."

"I hate it," she grumbled, then blew out a breath. "I'm sorry. I know I'm not the best company right now. And the physical therapist is supposed to be at the house in an hour. All I actually want to do is take a nap and then watch movies in bed for the rest of the night." She tapped a finger to the top of Wiley's hand. "I think I might need to reschedule the PT appointment."

"Nope." He shook his head. "It's set."

"I can call her back."

"But you won't," he insisted. "The only way to get stronger is to work at it."

She folded her arms across her middle, irritation crawling through her like an army of spiders. Wiley was right, of course, but that didn't mean Grace wanted to hear it. "I think I liked you better when you were bringing me flowers and being all sweet and romantic."

"We're saving sweet and romantic for after the therapy session," he promised. "Right now, I'm being your friend."

She opened her mouth, then shut it again, his words wiping away the irritation. As much as she enjoyed the kisses they shared, the thought of being Wiley's friend was just as appealing. "Friend or drill sergeant?" she asked, not bothering to hide the sarcasm from her voice. Sarcasm was an easy mask to hide behind.

"A little of both, actually." He pulled onto her parents' street. "Text me after the PT leaves, and I'm happy to come over or pick you up." He stopped at the curb. "Or if you just want a night alone with Netflix, I understand."

She snorted softly. "If it weren't for this stupid cast, I'd be all about the Netflix and chill with you."

He laughed. "We're in no hurry."

Those words splashed cold water on the flame that ignited inside her every time she thought about being with Wiley in an intimate way. Maybe there was no hurry, but they did have a built-in end date, and she'd do well to remember that.

"Sure," she whispered.

"Grace." He took her hand, and just that gentle touch sent shivers across her skin. "I mean it. No pressure."

Oh, heavens. He thought she was upset because he might be pushing her for something she wasn't ready to handle. What would he think if he knew that without the cast, she'd be tempted to crawl over the console and attach herself to him like a barnacle? Maybe not the most romantic image, but that's how she felt.

"I appreciate it," she answered, and placed her hand on the door handle. The thought of attaching any part of herself to Wiley had her feeling a bit unhinged. She was tired. And frustrated. And she wanted him more than she cared to admit. "I should go."

Wiley looked past her out the passenger window and gave a little wave. "Your mom is coming."

All thoughts of desire vanished into thin air. Grace sighed as her mother headed down the front walk toward them. She opened her door and called out a greeting as Wiley went around to the trunk of the car to retrieve her scooter.

"How was your day?" her mother asked as Grace climbed out.

"I texted you, Mom." She tried to keep the impatience out of her voice. "It was fine."

"You look tired."

"I'm fine."

"She's tired," Wiley confirmed. "After the physical therapy appointment, she should rest. If there's anything she needs—"

"I'll ask for it," Grace said through clenched teeth. She knew he was trying to be nice and she didn't want to take his generosity for granted, but being smothered with caring chafed at her, even if it was done with the best intentions.

Barbara bestowed a beaming smile on Wiley. "I appreciate you looking out for her. It makes me feel better about her going back to work before she's fully healed."

"It's my pleasure," Wiley answered. "Everyone at the hotel was happy to see her return."

"The photos you sent were adorable," her mother told him, reaching out to pat his arm.

Grace blinked. "Wait." She looked from her mom to Wiley. "You sent photos? You're texting my mother?"

"I asked him to, sweetheart," her mom explained. "I didn't want to bother you."

"So you bothered him instead?" Grace snapped, shaking her head.

"It was my pleasure," Wiley assured her.

"Not the point." Grace placed her purse and files into the scooter's basket with more force than was probably necessary. "I'm going into the house. Thank you for the ride, Wiley. I think after my appointment, I'll rest for the night after all."

His gaze clouded. "Whatever you want."

"Other than managing my own business," she muttered, and scooted toward the house as fast as she could manage.

"Gracie, don't be mad." Her mother caught up with her in a couple of quick steps. "Wiley was only doing what I asked. I know your father and I are overprotective, but you're our daughter. Please."

The catch in her mother's voice wound its way around Grace's heart. Of course she understood why her parents worried so much, even if she didn't like it. "I know, Mom," she said softly, pausing just before the front porch. "Give me a minute out here, okay?"

Barbara nodded and waved to Wiley before heading back into the house.

Grace turned the scooter, not a graceful move by any stretch of the imagination. As always, her breath caught at Wiley's pure physical perfection. She liked that he always dressed a touch more formally than his brothers, retaining his city polish even in Rambling Rose.

"You sent photos to my mom," she said, more a statement and less an accusation this time.

He took a step toward her and nodded.

She appreciated that he didn't try to make excuses or mansplain his behavior.

"I appreciate you looking out for me," she said quietly, looking down to the end of the block when the intensity of his gaze was too much. "But it's important to me that you understand I can take care of myself."

He moved closer slowly, as if approaching some feral creature. In truth, that's how Grace felt on the inside. Frustration and fatigue combined to sharpen her edges.

"I understand," he said. "You've proven yourself to be one of the most competent women I've ever known. You don't need my help, because you can handle anything."

"Right now it doesn't feel that way," she admitted. "It hasn't for a while. I let my prior relationship, and before that my family, dictate what I did in life. People around me were my priority, and I thought I had to put the needs of others before my own. I'm trying to change that." She reached down and massaged a hand along the top of her thigh. "Current circumstances aren't making it easy."

"I want to make it easier, Grace."

She studied him for a moment, the sophisticated attorney who seemed intent on making her feel special. It still boggled her mind that Wiley would be interested in a woman like her. In truth, that's part of why she resisted his involvement. She didn't want him to see her as a charity case.

"I don't mean to sound ungrateful." She crooked a finger, beckoning him closer. "I'm grateful for your help at the hotel. I'm grateful for you." When her voice threatened to crack, she swallowed back anything else she might say to him. Her feelings were too raw, too new at this point.

He laced their fingers together. "That goes both ways."

She felt a smile tug one corner of her mouth as butterflies fluttered across her stomach. "I want to kiss you right now, but we're standing on my parents' front lawn."

"Rain check?" he asked, leaning in close.

As an answer she brushed her lips over his, unable to resist. She drew back quickly, still cognizant of being on display for half the neighborhood. "I'll text you after my PT appointment."

The look of relief that filled his bourbon-hued gaze surprised her. It was as if he actually worried she might push him away. That he truly cared about her feelings.

He carried the scooter up the steps to the porch, and it was difficult to watch him walk toward his car again. Grace could imagine how much good it would do her exhausted spirit to spend an hour napping in Wiley's arms. But that certainly wasn't an option living with her parents.

It might be time for a change.

Chapter Eleven

Are you free for dinner?

Wiley blew out a relieved breath when Grace's simple text appeared on his phone screen the following afternoon. He'd gotten stuck on a series of conference calls with his Chicago colleagues that morning and then had a meeting at the county building inspector's office, so he didn't arrive at the hotel until after lunch. Grace had already left for home.

He couldn't tell why not seeing her for twenty-four hours made him feel anxious. Normally, Wiley set strict limits on his relationships so that the women he dated didn't get the wrong impression about his level of commitment.

Grace had practically accused him of trying to run her life yesterday, a clear sign that he was in too deep with her. He never got involved with women at that level. Flowers and other gifts—like the ones he'd given her after the accident—were…well, Wiley wouldn't describe them as meaningless. But they were superficial in a way that felt comfortable. He liked boundaries and limits. He liked control, especially after feeling he had so little of it as a kid in his overlarge blended family.

But the tiny town of Rambling Rose, and Grace in particular, made him want more.

He replied to the text that he'd pick her up at her parents' around six and received an immediate response with an unfamiliar address along with a message to come hungry for pizza.

The rest of the afternoon seemed to tick by in slow motion. He resisted the urge to google the address she'd sent him to see if they were meeting at a restaurant or something that would clue him in to her plan for the night. It occurred to Wiley that he might have a bit of an issue with control if he couldn't relinquish it long enough to allow Grace to surprise him with plans for the evening.

He left the hotel after checking progress on the balcony reconstruction. The painter had put the finishing touches on it, and the structure looked as good as new. Part of why Wiley had gone to the inspector's office was to discuss the possibility of sabotage in more detail. The man had assured him that they couldn't make a definite determination on what had caused the collapse. For now they believed the accident to be just that—an accident.

Wiley breathed a little easier at that news, although the cynic in him had a hard time totally trusting it. He would reserve judgment until the hotel opened without incident. But the relief on the faces of his brothers and sisters when he'd shared the news that the balcony may not have been tampered with made him want to believe. There was enough stress in putting the finishing touches on the hotel to have it ready for opening in less than a month. The idea that right now they wouldn't have to worry about sabotage on top of everything else clearly helped everyone. He also knew that the security system Kane had installed was top-notch. Nothing was going to get past them.

Anticipation continued to build in him as he drove to the ranch to change out of his suit and then headed back to town, following his car's GPS to the address Grace had given him. He parked in front of a nondescript brick fourplex in a residential neighborhood that he'd never been to before. Why would Grace have sent him there?

Frowning as he surveyed the block, Wiley was about to pull out his phone to text her when she called his name. He glanced toward the house to see Grace waving at him from a second-floor window.

"Come on up," she shouted. "I'll text you the code for the front door."

"How'd you get up there?" he asked as he approached the house.

She grinned, looking more relaxed than he'd seen her since that first night. "It's amazing what a girl can manage with the right motivation."

He entered the building, using the code that appeared on his phone. The converted house had two apartments on the first floor. The staircase that led to the second floor was narrow, and he couldn't imagine how Grace would have climbed the stairs. Obviously she'd made it to the second floor somehow.

She stood in the doorway of one of the upstairs apartments, looking more beautiful than ever in a simple sweater and a pair of loose sweatpants with the right leg cut off at the knee. Her hair was down around her shoulders, and although he'd seen her almost every day for the past week, there was something different about her tonight—a light in her eye that hadn't been there before.

"Welcome to my apartment," she said, backing up the scooter to give him room to enter. "It's not fancy, but guess what?" She took his hand as he entered and drew him close for a lingering kiss. "We're alone."

The thought sent a sensation surging through

him. He gave his body a silent command to settle down. Being alone with Grace didn't change anything. They were dating or friends or friends who were dating, depending on how he felt at any given moment.

"Why the change in location? Is everything okay with your family?" He squeezed her fingers. "I hope I didn't cause lingering problems between you and your mom because of updating her. Like I said—"

"Wiley, stop." She looked at him strangely, and he realized he was blathering. He wasn't a man who spoke compulsively or without prior thought. He chose his words deliberately, took action with purposeful thought. Wiley valued control above almost everything else, and suddenly one soft-spoken woman had turned everything he knew about himself on its side. "Everything is fine with my family." She shut the door behind him and released her hold on his hand, moving across the hardwood floor on the scooter toward the small kitchen positioned at the other end of the open space.

"Then why are you here?" He looked around the apartment and saw Grace's personality reflected in almost every part of it. It wasn't fancy, but from the row of bookshelves to the framed botanical posters above the slipcovered sofa, he could imagine her choosing every item with care. A complete contrast to his apartment in a sleek complex in downtown Chicago. He'd lived in his place for nearly seven years and had yet to hang a single piece of art on the walls.

The more time he spent in Rambling Rose, the more obvious it became that he was living life but hadn't created a home.

"I actually have you to thank once again," she said, grinning at him over her shoulder. "Thanks to your bullying, I didn't cancel the PT appointment yesterday."

"*Bullying* is such a harsh word," he told her with a grimace. "Can we use *support* or *encouragement*?"

"Bullying in the best way possible." She turned to him. "I needed it. You were right. Avoiding therapy wasn't going to help me heal faster or make anyone forget about the injury. The cast is kind of a give-away, you know?"

"That doesn't explain you moving back to a second-floor apartment."

"The therapist was wonderful. She gave me some exercises to help strengthen my leg muscles for the time I'm still in the cast. I explained to her how much trouble I'd been having with the crutches. She helped me learn to use them more effectively."

Grace pointed to the metal crutches that rested against the wall. "We even did some work on getting up and down stairs. Once I felt more confident, I knew I could move back here. I don't have to stay with my parents anymore."

"That's great." The radiant smile she gave him

did funny things to his heart. "And your folks are okay with it?"

Her smile dimmed slightly. "They aren't thrilled," she admitted, "but it's not their choice. My dad picked me up from work and drove me here this afternoon while Mom did some grocery shopping, so I won't starve." She opened the refrigerator to reveal the fully stocked shelves. "Once they saw that I could manage the stairs, it made them feel better about things. I need this so badly. I need to feel like I can make it on my own."

"Of course you can," he said because even though he didn't like to think of her struggling, he knew her independence was important to who she was, and he'd never take that from her. "You know I'll help with anything you need."

"Yeah," she whispered, biting down on her lower lip. "And I do have a few places that are achy."

He immediately took a step closer. "Have you been overdoing it at the hotel?"

She chuckled and tapped a finger to her mouth. "I hurt right here," she told him with a wink. "Any chance you'll kiss it and make it better?"

Every feeling of desire Wiley had locked down came roaring back to the surface. They were alone in her apartment. The thought of what it might mean made his body grow heavy with need.

Just as he reached her, the landline phone on the counter rang.

"Hold that thought." Grace pointed at him. "I think the pizza just arrived."

Food was the last thing Wiley cared about at the moment, but he opened the door for the delivery guy after Grace buzzed him into the building. To his surprise, she'd already paid over the phone, so all that was left for Wiley to do was hand the kid a couple of dollars as a tip.

"You don't have to buy me dinner," he told her as he carried the box to the two-seater kitchen table positioned in front of a window. "I'm the man. I should pay."

He wanted to slap himself as soon as the words left his mouth, and she flat out laughed at that statement. "You need to update your thoughts about relationships," she told him as she pulled two plates from the cupboard. "As much as I appreciate your gentlemanly tendencies, I'm a modern woman."

"I'm an ass," he muttered. "My mom and my sisters would kill me if they overheard that."

"Your intentions are noble."

"That's something, I guess. Are you sure you want to put up with me?"

She laughed again. "It's only for a couple—" He watched as she closed her eyes and drew in a deep breath. There was the reminder of his dwindling time in Texas, which was beginning to feel like a specter haunting the moments he shared with Grace.

So many things would be easier once he returned

to Chicago. Although Wiley was keeping up with his client load, working remotely meant everything seemed to take longer than it would if he were handling it at the main office. Despite that, he found he didn't want to think about leaving Rambling Rose or Grace. Especially Grace.

"Would you like a beer?" she asked when she met his gaze again, her eyes almost aggressively bright. "I had my mom pick up the same brand you ordered at dinner the other night."

"You're wining and dining me." He took the plates from her hand and leaned forward to kiss her neck, needing the sweet scent of her to ground him in the moment and help him forget the inevitable end to their time together. "I should push you out of your comfort zone more often."

Her shoulders relaxed, as though she appreciated his attempt to lighten the mood. "Be careful, Counselor," she warned, "or this modern woman might push your comfort zone right back."

Grace couldn't remember the last time she'd felt so content. It was nearly ten and she sat cradled in the crook of Wiley's arm as the final scene of an old sci-fi movie played on her small TV.

He was the first man she'd had in her apartment, and nerves had plagued her after she'd texted him the invitation earlier. She knew her place wasn't anything special, especially for a man who was probably used to living the high life in the city. Most of her furniture consisted of hand-me-downs from her parents or thrift-store finds. She'd shared a duplex apartment with her ex-boyfriend in Horseback Hollow and after discovering the depth of his betrayal, she'd been so intent on getting out of town, she'd simply left behind everything that wouldn't fit in her car.

It had only been a year since she'd returned to Rambling Rose, but her relationship with Craig seemed like a lifetime ago. It still amazed her how deeply she'd come to care for Wiley in such a short time. Maybe it was due to growing close to him in the aftermath of her accident, but Grace couldn't help but believe there was more to their connection.

If only she didn't keep getting the unwanted reminders that he'd be leaving sooner than later. She snuggled against him, reminding herself to stay in the moment instead of worrying about things she had no control over. That plan seemed to be serving her well as far as her job. Even though Jillian had found ways to remind Grace every day since her return about all the ways she wasn't contributing to progress toward the grand opening, Grace stayed focused on the pieces she could do. She'd invited owners of various local businesses, and plans for the Rambling Rose partnership reception were almost complete.

When the movie's credits rolled, Wiley dropped a gentle kiss on the top of her forehead. "This is nice," he said, one hand tracing lazy circles on her arm. The featherlight touch did funny things to her insides, her pulse thrumming at the thought of being truly alone with this irresistible man. Up until now, the only moments they'd had to themselves had been in his car, and there was only so much that could happen with a console separating them.

Not that a lot more could happen with her leg in the cast, but Grace tipped up her chin and trailed kisses along Wiley's strong jaw. His arms tightened around her, and he claimed her mouth, their tongues meeting as the kiss deepened. She wound her arms around his neck, reveling in the heat that surrounded her.

It felt like she could kiss him forever and never tire of it. Her body grew heavy with need and she shifted, wanting to get closer but not quite able to manage it with the cast hindering her.

"Are you okay?" he asked her when a frustrated sigh escaped her lips. "Am I hurting you? Is it your leg?"

She pulled back to gaze into his dark eyes. "I want more," she whispered. "What would the physical therapist think of me if I asked her how to manage…" She broke off and wrinkled her nose. "Being with you despite my cast."

One side of his mouth twitched. "I'm not sure, but I like the way your mind works." He smoothed a stray lock of hair from her face. "I like everything about you, Grace. So much so that I don't want to rush this."

As much as her brain appreciated his chivalry, Grace's body wasn't cooperating. "Will you stay with me tonight?" she asked, then felt heat rise to her cheeks at her own bluntness. Grace wasn't the type of woman to ask for what she wanted or take the lead in the bedroom. But it was different some-how with Wiley.

A thought wiggled its way into her mind. Maybe Wiley was being a gentleman because he didn't feel the same way about her. Although even her dad seemed to be warming to him, her brother still had suspicions about his motives. Jake still seemed to believe Wiley was protecting his family by getting close to her and sent her at least one text a day with some sort of veiled warning about not opening her heart to the Fortune attorney.

Grace didn't bother to tell Jake it was way too late for that. Her heart was already well in the mix.

She held her breath as she waited for Wiley's re-sponse. She could feel his heart beating a rapid-fire pace against his chest. "No pressure," she added when he didn't respond. "I'm not expecting anything to happen. Sleeping, of course. But otherwise—"

"Yes." He said the word with a level of rever-ence that sent shivers across her skin, then kissed her again.

By the time he finally pulled away, Grace felt dizzy with need.

"Don't ever doubt that I want you," he told her. "I do, Grace. So badly." He reached out and placed a hand on her leg just above the cast. "But not until you're healed totally. What I have planned for the two of us is going to be worth the wait. I promise."

"Okay," she said, her voice a squeak. How else could she answer?

She pushed away from him, needing a little bit of distance because she felt like she was in danger of spontaneously combusting. "I'm going to change into my pajamas and…" She covered her face with her hands. "This is weird, right? We're two adults—who are dating—and we're having a platonic sleepover. You must think I'm the biggest dork you've ever met."

"I think you're amazing," he assured her. He rose from the sofa, grabbed the remote to turn off the television and then extended his hands toward her.

She allowed him to pull her to standing but shook her head when he bent as if to pick her up. "I can make it to the bedroom on my own."

"Amazing," he repeated.

She laughed at that. "It's not far."

"I'm going to text Callum," Wiley said, "and tell them not to expect me home tonight."

She made a face. "Is that going to be weird?"

"I'm a grown man," he reminded her. "They might give me a little grief, but no one will be shocked."

As she made her way to the bedroom, Grace wasn't sure whether to be comforted or terrified by Wiley's comment. Did he make a habit of spending the night away from the ranch in beds that didn't belong to him?

No reason to go looking for trouble when it had a way of finding Grace without any prompting on her part. It only took a few minutes to change into her pj's and finish her nighttime routine.

Wiley was sitting on the edge of the bed when she came out of the bathroom. He'd taken off his sweatshirt and socks and shoes but still had on a T-shirt and jeans.

Somehow the sight of his bare feet on her rug made Grace's toes curl.

"Are you planning to sleep in your clothes?" she asked, trying for a light tone.

He shrugged. "I don't want to make you uncomfortable."

She kicked out her injured leg. "The cast beat you to it. It's okay, Wiley. I know nothing is going to happen between us, but I want you to get a decent night's sleep, as well."

He rose and approached her, running his hands up and down her arms. "Even if I don't sleep a wink, it will be worth it to spend the night holding you."

Damn, the guy knew what he was doing with the smooth talk.

She reached for his belt, slowly unbuckling it as she felt him watching her. "I'm glad to hear you say that. But drop trou, Mr. Fortune. I'm ready for bed."

He grinned at her teasing, and Grace felt her heart tug once more. She liked who she was with Wiley. He seemed willing to let her be who she was in a way that most people didn't appreciate, and that gave her the confidence to explore her inner strength.

Too bad she couldn't spend the whole night exploring him.

She climbed into bed and watched him undress, forcing herself not to whimper as he tugged off his T-shirt to reveal the most perfect physique she'd ever seen in person. He was lean and muscled, hard planes and angles on display in a way that reminded her of an actual sculpture. A smattering of dark hair covered his chest.

And he was going to spend the night with her.

He joined her under the covers, and she flipped off the light, then sighed with pleasure as he pulled her close. As much as she wanted him, there was something about the comfort of his arms around her that made the fatigue she tried to keep at bay rise up like a wave inside her.

"You can sleep, Grace," he said against her hair, as if he could sense her struggle to remain awake. "I'm not going anywhere."

She loved the sound of that, although she told herself not to forget that he meant he was with her for now. So for now she cuddled up against him and drifted off to sleep.

Chapter Twelve

The next week went by more quickly than Grace could have imagined. Between work at the hotel in the mornings and working at home on the business leaders' event during the afternoon hours, plus the physical therapy sessions and her time with Wiley, it felt like every minute was filled with something.

She'd never been happier.

It was strange that falling off the balcony seemed to be a catalyst for her newfound sense of confidence. Yet there was nothing like knowing she could have died to make her realize she needed to be willing to take more chances in life.

Grace had started to speak up more in meetings

and insert her ideas, not only for the opening, but for how she thought things would work best in the daily running of the hotel once they were filled with guests. To her surprise, the Fortunes seemed happy to let her take the lead, and she realized that the point of the training program might have been more than simply familiarizing locals with the business model. Because they were committed to hiring most of the hotel staff locally, the Fortune family needed a way to make sure whoever they chose was going to be up for the job.

Grace and Jillian had similar backgrounds and experience in hospitality, but they had very different methods for how to deal with guests and the hotel's overall ambiance. Jillian clearly felt as though it should be an exclusive oasis that would cater to big-city guests from Houston or other parts of the state who wanted to get away from the pressures of city life but still retain the trappings of privilege. Grace saw the value in that, but because she'd grown up in Rambling Rose, she also understood what the town had to offer. Her idea was to capitalize on the community feel. Yes, the hotel was an escape but one that guests would choose in part because of the charm of the surrounding area.

It's why her Rambling Rose partnership reception felt so important. She wanted local business owners to buy in on the hotel so that when it opened and guests came to town, the community would welcome them in a way that would make people want to return over and over.

"Am I interrupting?"

The soft knock on the office door had her glancing up from her laptop. She grinned as Wiley entered, looking handsome as ever in his dark suit and crisp white tailored shirt.

"You're never an interruption," she told him, feeling the familiar rush of heat that rose to her cheeks whenever Wiley spoke to her. Since she moved back to her apartment, he'd been over almost every evening for dinner. He didn't always spend the night but stayed long enough to kiss and caress her until her body was on fire with wanting more.

"You have the office to yourself this morning?" He gestured toward the other workstations situated around the perimeter of the room. All of the employees involved with the trainee program shared this space, which would be the official management office once the hotel opened.

"Jillian and Jay are in a meeting upstairs to finalize the choice for bed linens for the guest rooms." She shrugged. "I had a call with Hailey at the spa about the giveaways for the preopening event. I figured they could handle it without me."

"Look at you delegating like you've already earned the promotion." He bent down and gave her a swift kiss. "I like watching you take control."

As much as she wanted to draw him in, Grace

gave him a playful nudge instead. "You can't kiss me at work," she admonished. "People will talk."

"There's no one here."

"Still." She held up a hand. "And I'm not delegating. We're dividing and conquering."

He lifted a brow. "Own it, Grace. You want that promotion, and you're going after it."

"Yeah," she whispered, delighted that she didn't have to hide her ambition from Wiley. Her ex hadn't liked it when she tried to better herself, at least if it made her seem like she was trying to surpass him in any way. Maybe it was because Wiley was already so successful and sure of himself, but he seemed to be attracted to her even more when she stood up for herself or went after what she wanted.

It was a heady vote of confidence.

"Saturday's event is going to be great." She grinned and pushed away from her computer. "Do you know what's going to make it even better?"

Wiley tapped a finger against his chin. "The fact that every time we make eye contact you'll know that I'm thinking about kissing you senseless?"

She laughed. "No, but I'll keep that in mind. I get the cast off Friday afternoon."

His mouth dropped open and something flashed in his eyes that she didn't understand—it looked almost like dismay. "I thought you had a full month in the cast?"

"Me, too. But I saw Dr. Matthews early this morning. My mom took me in before work. He did more scans and said the fracture is healing faster than expected. The plan was to make an appointment for next week to get it off, but when I explained about the event on Saturday, he agreed to see me Friday afternoon. I'll still have to be in a walking boot for another few weeks, but…" She threw up her hands. "Walking, Wiley. Without crutches or the scooter. I'm going to almost be a normal person again."

"That's fantastic news." He continued to look shocked and definitely not thrilled the way she expected. "Are you sure you aren't pushing the recovery? What does the PT say?"

"Wow, that's not exactly the reaction I'd hoped for," Grace told him with a frown. "The doctor is okay with it, so I don't think I'm pushing anything. We already have physical therapy sessions set up for next week to start working on strengthening my ankle." She didn't bother to keep the frustration out of her voice. "This is a huge step forward—literally and figuratively—and comes at the best possible time. Not just because of work." She swallowed. "I mean you and I can…well, we'll be free to take the next step in our relationship."

He sucked in a sharp breath. "Yes. That's amazing." He waved a hand in the air, looking so discombobulated she almost felt sorry for him. "Every part of it is amazing, Grace. I'm really so happy for you. It's just a shock, you know? Because the plan changed and all."

"For the better," she reminded him.

"Of course."

Jillian entered the office in her usual flourish, then stopped when she realized Wiley was standing next to Grace's chair. "Thank God I was at that meeting."

He took a step back and ran a hand through his hair.

"Nice work with arranging the spa gift certificate," he told Grace with a perfunctory nod.

She gave him a wan smile, hoping that Jillian was fooled by his somewhat lame attempt to offer a reason for being in here with her. She wished they didn't have to keep their relationship secret, but until the promotion was announced, she wouldn't take any chances on her coworkers thinking she would be given preferential treatment during the assessment process.

Even being with him in secret felt risky, but she also couldn't imagine not taking advantage of their time together.

"Nice to see you, Jillian," Wiley said, and for a moment Grace hoped Wiley wasn't a poker player, because the man's inability to display a convincing game face was comical.

He exited the office as Jillian took a seat at her desk.

"The linen meeting went well?" Grace asked, knowing that the other woman loved to talk about herself and hoping she'd be easily distracted from Wiley's presence in the office.

"If it weren't for me, our guests would have been sleeping on discount sheets and scratchy comforters." Jillian opened her laptop. "The bedding company sales guy was definitely trying to pull something over on us."

"What did Jay think?" Grace valued his practical opinion to balance out Jillian's tendency toward drama.

"He actually agreed with me." Jillian sounded as shocked as Grace felt. "I would not have expected Jay to be the type of man who understood the value of Egyptian cotton or a high thread count. He seems like a guy who'd change his sheets once a month and only because he got sick of crumbs in the bed."

"Yuck." Grace shook her head. "You're selling him a little short."

"He's just so regular," Jillian said with a sniff. "Nice enough but definitely not someone with my level of ambition."

Grace inclined her head. "I hate to ask where I rate on your ambition scale, but I'm curious."

Jillian steepled her hands together as she turned her chair fully to face Grace. "Well, you take it to a whole new level."

That didn't sound like a compliment, so Grace offered her best placating smile. As much as she wanted to earn the promotion, there was no doubt that Jillian would be an asset to the hotel staff in some capacity, so Grace didn't want to be the woman's sworn enemy. "You do a great job as well," she said.

"But I don't do the boss's brother," Jillian said with a smirk. "I earn my accolades with hard work and talent."

Anger and alarm rose in Grace like two waves crashing in on each other. This was exactly why she'd been leery of dating Wiley before the grand opening. The fact that Jillian could even hint—let alone nearly accuse—Grace of being given some kind of preferential treatment pained her to the core.

"I don't know what you're talking about," she said, making sure not one bit of emotion seeped into her voice. "Wiley and I are friends. He was kind after the accident."

"I assume you repaid that kindness on your back?" Jillian asked, almost conversationally.

Grace gasped. "That's a horrible thing to say."

"But is it true?"

"No, it's not. I don't appreciate the insinuation about my character. I've earned my place at the Hotel Fortune."

"He's only friendly to you because they're afraid you're going to sue for damages or try to get some kind of settlement from the hotel."

"That's not true," Grace whispered even as her

brother's words played over in her head like an annoying refrain. She reminded herself that Jillian wanted to get under her skin, and Grace had to keep it together. She knew Wiley truly cared about her. He told her as much—maybe not in so many words, but the way he held her communicated everything she needed to know.

"I overheard him talking to Callum and Nicole right after the accident." Jillian stood and moved closer to Grace's workstation. "He told them that he'd 'handle you.' We all know what that means when an attorney says those words."

"You're lying."

"I'm not. Ask him if you want. But men like Wiley Fortune don't fall for small-town girls like you, Grace. He's not even staying in Rambling Rose, so if you can't see that you're just an easy distraction with the added benefit that he protects his family, then you're even stupider than I suspected." She pressed her glossy lips together. "I feel sorry for you, actually. I have a friend who works at Cowboy Country and she told me how you were publicly humiliated by your boyfriend up there. Some people can't ever learn the lesson."

Without waiting for a response, Jillian turned and left the room.

Grace stared blankly at her computer screen as her body began to tremble. Was it possible Jillian had told her the truth? The woman was conniving and egotistical, but Grace had never once heard her lie in the months they'd worked together.

She hadn't understood Wiley's reaction to her news about the cast coming off early. Maybe he liked having an excuse not to be intimate with her. He'd given her too many reasons to believe he was a gentleman for her to doubt him on that front. It would then make sense if he was really stringing her along or getting close to her to make sure she didn't go after his family for the accident that he wouldn't want things to go too far.

As many times as Grace had warned herself not to let her feelings for him get out of control, that's exactly what had happened. She was falling for Wiley Fortune—falling in love with him. And now she feared she might end up with a broken heart and a betrayal that would hurt far worse than Craig's. If Wiley was the man Jillian claimed him to be, Grace wasn't sure if she'd ever recover.

The following morning Wiley walked toward a popular barbecue joint in downtown Austin where he was meeting his cousin Gavin for lunch. Gavin was the youngest son of Kenneth, the half brother of Wiley's dad. Similar to Wiley's branch of the clan, Gavin's was a big family who hadn't known about their connection to the famous Texas Fortunes until the past few years. Gavin and his siblings had grown up in Texas. Like Wiley, Gavin was an attorney and specialized in corporate law.

They hadn't met, but Wiley knew his cousin worked for a prominent firm out of Austin. It was Wiley's understanding that Gavin had transferred there from Denver when he decided to return permanently to Texas.

After the conversation with Grace yesterday, Wiley had reached out and asked to meet Gavin to discuss possible opportunities within his firm.

The news that Grace was getting her cast off early had been a shock, and he knew he hadn't handled it well. But that wasn't due to the reasons Grace might suspect. In truth, the thought of making love to her appealed to him more than he could say. He wanted to learn every inch of her body and how she liked to be touched, what he could do to bring her pleasure. He'd forced himself to put fantasies about the two of them to the side out of respect for her recovery. It had been an exquisite torture to kiss her and hold her in his arms each night when he stayed at her apartment and know that they couldn't go any further.

But a part of him, a tiny rational sliver of his brain, appreciated having the cast as an excuse not to take things further. Grace was different from any other woman he'd dated. He suspected that being with her intimately, instead of quenching his thirst, would only make him want her more.

The thought of taking that step and then walking

away after the hotel's grand opening made a sharp ache slice across his chest. The alternative—a long-distance relationship—held no appeal, either. Because of that, Wiley had decided to think about his future in a new way.

He immediately spotted Gavin as he entered the restaurant since he'd read his cousin's bio on the firm's website. Gavin was tall and good-looking, with dark blond hair and air of confidence about him. He waved and then gave Wiley's hand a firm shake when he got to the table.

"I'm glad you called," his cousin said, and Wiley appreciated the open expression on the other man's face.

"Thanks for being willing to meet me so quickly." He took a seat, and a waitress put a glass of water and a menu in front of him. "It's strange to think our fathers are brothers but we're virtual strangers."

Gavin nodded. "My dad had a bit of struggle getting used to being part of the Fortune clan."

"I know how that goes," Wiley said with a laugh. His father had actively discouraged Callum and the rest of the siblings from getting close to their new-found relatives. "But it's a hard family to resist."

"How do you like Rambling Rose?" Gavin asked. "From everything I hear, your siblings are making quite the mark on that little town."

"It's growing on me," Wiley admitted, glancing at the menu. "Which I didn't expect."

The waitress returned to take their orders. After she'd gone, Gavin sat back in his seat with a contented sigh. "I'm familiar with that, as well. I certainly hadn't planned to end up in Texas when I came for my sister's wedding. Denver had been my home since I graduated from law school."

"So what changed?" Wiley leaned in, curious to get the insight of a man who on the surface appeared so like him. "Did the wide-open spaces of Texas call you home again?"

"Not exactly. There's plenty of space in Colorado, although it's certainly not the same. The truth is, I met a woman. It's as simple as that."

Wiley chuckled. "In my experience, women are never simple."

"The way I felt about Christine is." Gavin inclined his head. "Although it took me a bit of time to figure it out. I might be great with contract law, but I wasn't exactly a quick study when it came to love. Luckily, my firm had a Austin office, so it was easy to transfer without missing a beat. Best decision I ever made."

"I don't have your luck," Wiley told the other man, still reeling at the fact that Gavin seemed to be acting like it had been no big deal to make that kind of a move for a relationship. "How long have you and Christine been together?"

"Two years this month," Gavin told him with a

smile. "Smartest thing I ever did was make her my wife. We'll be adding to our family this spring."

"Congratulations." Wiley rubbed two fingers against his chest, wondering if the emotion there that felt like jealousy could actually be that base. It wasn't as if he'd completely rejected the idea of someday getting married and having a family of his own. But having his own space and independence had always been more of a priority. As much as he appreciated the sacrifices his mom and stepdad had made, he didn't know if he was capable of being that selfless.

"It's incredible. Christine is incredible. I really am the luckiest damn man alive."

The waitress brought their food at that moment—brisket for Wiley and a pulled pork sandwich for Gavin. As they ate, Gavin asked Wiley about his work in Chicago and how he was able to balance everything remotely from Rambling Rose. They discussed Gavin's transition to Texas and what that had meant for his career and his standing in the firm.

Before this month, Wiley had never considered that he might want a change from the firm where he was on the fast track to partner. He'd made a life in Chicago that suited him, although he was quickly coming to realize his desire to stay in Rambling Rose was more than just a need for a break from the pace of city life.

He wanted a change.

As if reading his thoughts, Gavin gave him a knowing look across the table. "You've told me everything I need to know about your focus as an attorney," his distant cousin said. "Obviously you've had a lot of success in your career and from the sound of it, you have a great life in Chicago. Yet you called to discuss opportunities with my firm in Austin?"

As ridiculous as it seemed, Wiley's first instinct was to deny it. No point, since that's exactly why he had called Gavin, but saying the words out loud felt monumental, like he'd be making a huge shift from the path that had always seemed solid in front of him.

"I think it might be time to consider other opportunities," he answered slowly. "I've enjoyed reconnecting with my brothers and sisters. Somehow being part of a big family doesn't quite feel as stifling as it once did. Now it's more of a comfort, and I like the idea of being able to help out legally with what they're doing in Rambling Rose. But I'm not ready to give up corporate law. I'd like to find a way to do both."

Gavin studied him for several long beats. "You want to move to Texas permanently to be closer to your family?"

"Yes."

"That's the only reason?" Gavin prompted.

"I'm ready for a new challenge." Wiley kept his features neutral. He could tell the other man wanted something more, a revelation about love or a woman.

But Wiley wasn't ready for that. The idea of taking his relationship with Grace to the next level had certainly contributed to his desire to explore new opportunities in Texas. She wasn't the type of woman he would expect to have a casual relationship.

Yes, they'd agreed to date temporarily while he was in town, but that arrangement had been made while she was at the beginning of her recovery. He hadn't expected his feelings for her to grow so deep in such a short time. The idea of making love to her and then walking away after the grand opening held no appeal. Even if he wasn't ready to talk to her yet about his emotions, he needed to be moving forward. The thought of living permanently in Texas helped him to retain some level of control.

"I'd like to set up a meeting with you and one of the senior partners," Gavin told him. "Our Austin office is continuing to expand, and it would be a huge win to attract an associate with your level of experience." He leaned forward. "Are you thinking of living in Austin, or do you want to stay close to your family in Rambling Rose?"

"Rambling Rose," Wiley said without hesitation. He knew what working at the hotel meant to Grace. Although Austin wasn't far, he'd grown accustomed to being able to see her every night. He liked having dinner with her and hearing about her day and sharing the details of his. He'd always been serious and analytical, comfortable with seeing the world through his view alone. Her mind worked in a different way than his did, and it fascinated him.

"Okay, then." Gavin nodded. "Let's see what we can do to make this happen."

Wiley released a breath he hadn't realized he was holding. Moving forward with a potential relocation to Texas permanently made him feel like he could take the next step with Grace with no reservations. And his body and his heart wanted that next step in equal measure.

Chapter Thirteen

Grace stared at her left ankle as if she'd never seen it before. The feeling of air on her skin after so long was both strange and exhilarating. Although her un-injured leg hadn't gotten any exposure to the winter sun, the skin on her newly exposed leg looked par-ticularly sallow and a bit pinched. It felt odd to be able to move her foot. Her entire body felt lighter without the weight of the cast.

"You're sure it's time?"

The orthopedic surgeon chuckled. "Normally my patients don't second-guess me when I remove a cast. They're too busy thanking me."

She placed a hand over her face and gave him an

embarrassed smile. "I'm sorry, Doctor. Of course I trust you. You're the expert. It's just such a surprise to have it happening earlier than I expected. Now I just need a shower and to shave my legs."

"You're young and healthy," he said with a chuckle. "The body is a miraculous healer, and yours did an amazing job at it. Let's not get ahead of ourselves. You'll still need to wear the walking boot for another month. Physical therapy is going to be critical to strengthen the ankle. I know you've gone back to work, which is fine, but I don't want you to overdo it."

"I won't," she promised. "I'll be careful. I'm just so excited to not have to use the crutches or the scooter."

"I'm happy to be able to help you."

"What about driving?" Grace said, still marveling at the thrill of being able to return to a somewhat normal life.

"I would say take it slow." The doctor typed in a few notes on his laptop as he spoke. "And no standard transmission. The boot and a clutch aren't going to be a good mix. But if the car is an automatic, then I see no issue."

"I get my life back," Grace said on a happy sigh.

"Listen to your body," he advised. "If you need to rest, do that. I mean it, Grace. I know that you're driven and motivated. We want to see the progress you've made so far continue."

"Got it. Thank you so much."

They finished up the appointment, and she scheduled a follow-up with the desk. The boot was awkward, but not nearly as cumbersome as the cast had been. Grace smiled as she walked out to the reception area where her mother and brother were waiting.

"No more cast," her mother said and enveloped Grace in a tight hug. "This is fantastic, Gracie."

Jake playfully ruffled her hair. "I was getting ready to put a bell on your scooter. It slowed you down at bit."

"No more time for slow," she said, then glanced over her shoulder. She didn't need the doctor to overhear her. Of course, she wasn't going to push it, but Grace felt more than ready to get back to regular life. Especially when that involved taking her relationship with Wiley to the next level. "I even get to drive."

"You behind the wheel is scary on a good day," Jake said with a chuckle.

Grace narrowed her eyes. "Not helpful."

They walked out into the medical center parking lot. "I need to stop at the grocery store on the way home," Barbara said, turning to Grace. "Do you want to go with me? Or Jake can give you a ride to your apartment."

"I'd like to get back," Grace said. "Wiley is coming for dinner so—"

"Seriously?" Jake bit back a groan. "Isn't it time to

cut the cord with that guy? You're basically healed. You don't need him keeping tabs on you anymore."

"Jake, be nice," their mother said gently.

"Or just be quiet," Grace added.

"I still don't trust him." Jake lowered his mirrored sunglasses to look at Grace. "I'm sure he'll be doing a happy dance now that you don't seem to have any long-term, potentially expensive injuries for his family to take care of."

"Wiley has been kind to your sister." Barbara smiled. "He's a good friend."

Jake sniffed but Grace held up a hand when he would have argued with their mother. "It's my life, Jake. I get to live it how I see fit. Maybe I'll go to the grocery store with Mom just so I don't have to listen to you."

"Come on, Gracie." He looped an arm around her shoulder. "Let me drive you home. I won't talk any more about the Fortunes."

"Call if you need anything," her mother said. "I expect you both at the house for Sunday supper." She patted Grace's arm. "Bring your Wiley if you'd like, sweetie. We can all get to know each other better."

"Thanks, Mom. Love you." Grace gave her mother a final hug, then followed Jake to his truck. She didn't like the tense silence that had fallen between them. She and Jake had always been close, even more so when she returned home to help after his car accident.

"Will you give Wiley a chance?" she asked softly

as her brother pulled out of the medical center parking lot.

"Is it actually serious between the two of you?"

She bit down on the inside of her cheek, unsure how to answer that question. From the standpoint of her heart, it certainly felt serious. Although it had only been a few weeks since they'd met, she could hardly imagine her life before Wiley or how she'd kept herself occupied. At the same time, she knew he was leaving, so it wouldn't make sense to become too attached. The sharp ache in her heart told her it might be too late for that.

"I like him," she said, because that was the truth without revealing too much. "I'm not expecting whatever is going on between us to continue after he leaves, although I wouldn't be opposed to a long-distance relationship."

"Really?" Jake's fingers tightened on the steering wheel. "I know I'm rough on him, Grace, but it's because I don't want to see you get hurt." He glanced over at her. "You didn't talk much about the breakup with Craig, but it obviously was hard on you."

She ran a finger along the seam of her jeans. "The hardest thing about Craig was that he cheated on me and humiliated me in front of everyone we worked with at Cowboy Country."

"Snake," Jake muttered. "I still wish you would have let me pay him a visit."

"Stop trying to sound like you're auditioning

for a gangster movie," she said with an affectionate chuckle. Although she and Jake might argue, there was no doubt her brother would do anything to protect her, and she appreciated his unwavering loyalty. "Wiley isn't like Craig."

"He's an attorney," Jake said with a derisive smirk. "If you look up the word in the dictionary, there might be a picture of a snake next to the definition."

"You have to trust me. Wiley isn't like that. He's honorable. I might not be able to adequately explain our connection or how instantaneous it was, but I know it doesn't have anything to do with my injury." Her gut tightened as she remembered Jillian's nasty comments about Wiley's motivations for being with Grace. She tried to put her rival's suspicions out of her head, chalking them up to jealousy or Jillian's attempts to undermine Grace's confidence.

"I do trust you. But the verdict's still out on the Fortune."

"Jake." As he pulled in front of her apartment building, Grace reached across the console and flicked his arm the way she used to do when they were kids. "Come on. Even Dad had a civil conversation with him a few days ago."

"I'm glad you're happy, Gracie." Her brother shrugged. "Can that be enough for now?"

"For now." She opened the car door and climbed out.

"I'd ask if you need help, but I already know the answer. Call or text if that changes."

"I will." Grace turned. "You're going to come to my event tomorrow, right?"

"The one where Fortunes will be crawling all over the place?" Jake grimaced.

"The one where you'll be supporting your favorite sister," Grace countered.

Jake gave a mock shudder but nodded. "I'll be there."

Grace waved as he pulled away, then headed upstairs. She wasn't going to win any sprinting contests with the boot, but it was a lot easier to manage the staircase without crutches. She checked her watch as she let herself into her apartment. The doctor's appointment had taken longer than she expected, so she only had an hour until Wiley was scheduled to arrive.

Her plan to go to the grocery store on her own for the first time since the accident so she could make him a proper home-cooked dinner would have to be saved for another night. Once again, she put aside thoughts of how few nights they might have left together. What would Wiley think if she proposed attempting to continue their relationship across the miles?

She got undressed, undid the Velcro straps on the walking boot and climbed into the shower as she considered that option. For her, a long-distance romance wouldn't be enough, but she'd be willing to try. Anything so that Wiley could remain a part of her life. He seemed to truly enjoy Rambling Rose, and she knew he loved spending more time with his siblings, so maybe he'd be in favor of visiting Texas on a more regular basis.

Hope and trepidation battled silently inside her at the thought of what their future might hold.

Her phone pinged as she came out of the bathroom, a series of texts from Callum with a minor crisis regarding the setup for tomorrow's event. Grace didn't hesitate to begin making calls and sending off messages from her laptop to mitigate any potential issues. A few months ago, she wasn't sure she would have had the confidence to take charge without an internal panic attack plaguing her. Her time in the training program and working toward the goal of the manager promotion had taught her a lot about herself and what she was capable of handling.

Unfortunately, when the knock sounded on her apartment door, Grace realized she'd lost track of time. Instead of putting on a nice outfit and hoping to impress Wiley before a potential next step in their relationship, she made her way to the door in a fuzzy polka-dot robe with her still-damp hair loose around her shoulders. She didn't even bother to put on a dab of lip gloss. What was the point? She'd messed up this night before it even started.

* * *

Wiley sucked in a breath and tried to control his rapidly beating heart when Grace smiled at him as she opened the door to her apartment.

He wasn't sure what he'd expected, but Grace in a soft bathrobe—and possibly nothing more—with her damp hair cascading over her shoulders and a pink glow tingeing her cheeks definitely was more than he bargained for.

"Sorry," she said immediately, taking a step back to let him enter. "I had to take care of something for tomorrow and lost track of—"

She let out a small yelp when he scooped her into his arms, kicking shut the door with one foot. He claimed her mouth with an urgency he hadn't realized he felt until that moment. The entire drive back from Austin, Wiley had been weighing in his mind the pros and cons of making a permanent move to Texas.

Was it too much? Too soon? Would he lose the independence and autonomy he'd carved out in his life like he was sculpting it from precious marble if he gave up his life in Chicago?

But seeing Grace made him understand in an instant that he wouldn't be giving up anything. In fact, it felt like he'd be moving toward something, claiming a future he hadn't imagined for himself. One that now felt like it was his destiny.

He wondered if the woman in his arms might be his destiny.

"You are beautiful," he told her as he trailed kisses along her neck. She smelled clean, like soap and lemons, a combination that had his senses reeling.

"I didn't even do my hair," she said with a laugh that quickly turned into a moan as he nipped at the sensitive place under her earlobe.

"Your hair is perfect," he said, sifting his fingers through the silky strands. "Tell me you aren't wearing anything under this robe."

He felt more than heard the hitch in her breath. "Nothing."

"Thank God," he murmured, then forced himself to pause. She wasn't trying to seduce him, he knew, or be purposely tempting the way some women would. Wiley wanted her all the more because of it.

But he also wanted to respect a pace that made her comfortable. Until he talked to his boss back in Chicago and the senior partners from Gavin's firm in Austin, he wasn't ready to discuss a potential move with her. He had to make sure everything was going to work out before he made any commitments or promises to Grace.

A little voice niggled at the corner of his mind, one that warned him love wasn't something he could control or put in a neat little box the way Wiley liked to do with the pieces of his life. But he shoved that warning into a dark corner. This was new territory for him, even being willing to consider a change in his life for another person. He wasn't quite ready to make the jump without knowing he had a solid place to land on the other side.

He would give her at least that same consideration. "Do you want to talk about the issue for tomorrow?" he asked as he put her down, then gripped her arms and shifted her away from him. The robe had loosened as they'd embraced, and he tried not to look at the expanse of soft skin he could see in the deep vee where it gaped.

She gave him a strange look, although her eyes were still cloudy with desire. "I handled it."

"Of course," he agreed. "How is your ankle?" He leaned down to take in the black walking boot that covered her leg from midcalf to foot. "Your text said the doctor thinks everything is healing properly?"

"Properly," she repeated, and he heard something in her tone that sounded like amusement. He couldn't figure out what was funny about the struggle to be a gentleman instead of continuing to ravish her the way he wanted to.

"Are you hungry?" He glanced over her shoulder toward the kitchen. She'd mentioned making dinner, but by the looks of the clean counters it seemed as though they might be going out. That was fine. He could wait to kiss her—and more. He could wait as long as needed.

"Wiley." She reached out and cupped his cheek

in her palm. He leaned in, soothed as always by her touch. "Did you hear the part where I said I'm naked under my robe?"

He swallowed and locked his knees as his legs suddenly went weak. "Yes."

"And your reaction is that you want to talk about the hotel event or my ankle or dinner?"

"I want to not take advantage of..." He licked his lips. "You lost track of time. The part about the robe...and you being..." Words abandoned him for a few moments as he struggled to retain control. "I don't want to rush you, Grace."

The corner of her mouth twitched, and he would have given anything to read her thoughts at the moment.

"I don't want to rush, either."

He felt his eyes go wide as she hooked her thumb in the robe's thick sash and undid it.

"In fact..." Her smile widened. "I hope that what comes next takes us all night." Then she pushed the robe off her shoulders.

Grace waited for Wiley's reaction to her bold move with her heart practically beating out of her chest. She wasn't normally one to make the first move—or any move—and certainly not to be assertive when it came to intimacy.

Her ex-boyfriend had been her first and only partner, and their intimacy had always been more about his pleasure than hers. She figured that was simply how it worked for a woman like her. As Craig had told her when she confronted him about his cheating, there were women men dated because they made good girlfriends and women men wanted because they were desirable.

He'd left no question that Grace fell into the former category.

But she wanted more from Wiley—with Wiley. She wanted more from herself and was quickly learning that the best way to achieve what she wanted was to take risks.

Standing naked in front of a man who looked like he belonged in some sort of catalog for genetic lottery winners, the lower part of one leg still encased in an orthopedic boot, definitely felt like a risk.

One she realized was worth it when Wiley's dark gaze traveled over her body, and his chest began to rise and fall in ragged breaths.

"I never expected..." He broke off, gave a small shake of his head and reached for her.

"Me, neither," she said against his mouth as he drew her close, his warm hands splayed across her bare back and bottom.

He muttered a curse low in his throat as he lifted her into his arms. "I can't wait," he said. "I want you so badly, Grace. I've wanted you since that first moment I saw you at the hotel."

She wrapped her arms tight around his neck, inhaling his scent as sensation swirled through her. She should feel vulnerable. After all, she was completely exposed while he remained fully dressed. But instead, she felt powerful in a way she didn't recognize. Like she was finally claiming a part of herself that had been waiting for her to realize it was important.

Wiley gave her the confidence to step into the woman she was meant to be.

He paused when he came to the door of her bedroom.

"I want you, too," she told him, brushing a kiss over his lips. "No more waiting, Wiley. We're in this together."

"Together," he repeated on a rush of air.

He pulled down the covers and placed her on the bed with exquisite care.

But when he reached for the strap of her boot, she placed her hand over his.

"You have too many clothes on," she told him with a smile.

"Easily remedied." He stood without hesitation, loosened his tie and then unbuttoned his shirt, pausing halfway through. "My fingers are shaking," he told her with an almost shy smile. "That's what you do to me."

Heat infused every part of her body at the thought of having an effect on this man.

Then her chest tightened as he continued to divest himself of his clothes, and Grace realized that they were truly taking the next step in their relationship. Sex meant something to her, and a moment of panic broke through the desire filling her brain, at the re- alization that she was embarking on this act with a man who might willingly walk away from her.

As he sat on the edge of the bed and placed a gentle hand on her booted leg, she realized it didn't matter. She might want more than they'd agreed to at the beginning of their time together, but she had to believe that he wanted it, too.

There might not be words yet, but the tenderness of his touch and the intensity of his gaze on hers were enough to make her trust that she was choos- ing the right path.

He undid the straps of the boot and slipped it off her leg. "Is this okay?" he asked softly, then bent to place a soft kiss on the top of her knee. "I don't want to hurt you, Grace. I'd never purposely hurt you."

"It's fine," she said, surprised when emotion clogged her throat. She didn't want to read more into his words. She knew he wouldn't hurt her deliberately, but she also understood that didn't mean she wouldn't end up with a broken heart.

But as his hand moved across her skin and he kissed a path up her body, nothing else mattered. He lavished attention on all the most sensitive parts of her, like he wanted to memorize her with his tongue and fingers.

"Stay still, sweetheart," he whispered against her. "We're going to be gentle with your ankle."

Gentle was the last thing on Grace's mind, but she did her best not to writhe under his kisses. It felt as though he was undoing her, desire thrumming through her like the crest of a wave. The pressure built inside her as he continued to explore her body, and minutes—or hours—later he drove her to the edge and over, and a cry broke from her lips.

Still it wasn't enough. As mind-blowing as her release had been, she wanted more. She wanted all of him. It might only be for now, the time he was in town, but Grace wouldn't consider that. All she knew was at this moment, they were meant to be together.

"Now, Wiley," she said. "I need you now."

"I'm here," he told her, and captured her mouth. "More."

He pulled away and reached for his wallet on her nightstand and pulled out a condom. A few moments later he was poised between her legs, and Grace had never wanted anything more than she wanted this man inside her.

His hands were braced on either side of her head and he entered her in one long stroke. She breathed him in and then lifted her head to kiss him, needing to be joined with him as much as she could manage.

Her eyes drifted closed as the rhythm of their kiss synced with the motion of their bodies. They moved together like they were built for each other, and in some ways Grace wondered if that were the truth. Had she been made for this man? Had everything that had come before led to the moment when their eyes met across that crowded party?

Because she'd never been certain what her place in the world was, but there was no doubt she'd found where she belonged in Wiley Fortune's arms.

He whispered little nothings into her ear between kisses, his hands holding her like she was the most precious thing in the world to him. Passion skyrocketed inside her until it felt like electricity coursed through her veins. She wasn't certain how much more pleasure she could take. The depth of it was like nothing she'd ever experienced.

And then she fell over the cliff she'd been racing toward, her body dissolving as if it were made of champagne bubbles fizzing into the air. Her body tightened around Wiley and a few seconds later, he cried out her name.

It was the most amazing thing she'd ever heard. They might not have made promises to each other with words, but Grace had no doubt that his body had just pledged something to her that guaranteed she would never be the same.

Had she been about to thank him? Had she been
ashamed of kissing him back—

Chapter Fourteen

"The timing couldn't be worse," Wiley muttered
as he packed his suitcase the following morning.

Megan flopped onto his bed in the suite where he
was staying at the ranch. He'd been as skeptical about
the property as he had about his siblings settling
in Rambling Rose when he'd first come to Texas.
The idea of his brothers and sisters living together
seemed like a recipe for disaster to Wiley, who had
far too many memories of their bustling house growing up and never being able to get a moment's peace.

But the arrangement worked—surprisingly—in
large part because the setup of the house allowed
whoever was living there to have their own private

space while still being under the same roof. He'd enjoyed reconnecting with his siblings on a daily basis, sharing coffee in the morning and whatever was on the menu for dinner.

The ranch employed a caretaker, who took care of most things, including meals, although Nicole and Megan took their turns in the kitchen because they found great pleasure in feeding the people they loved.

Wiley wondered if his memories of childhood weren't exactly accurate. Had he been the only one to feel stifled by their crowded, sometimes overbearing family? Or had he just been so committed to finding his own way and establishing an identity away from his successful stepfather and the rest of the family that he'd gone too far in the other direction?

"You'll be back for the grand opening though?" she asked, her tone sympathetic.

"Yes." He zipped shut the suitcase. "Well before that, I hope. I'm not sure exactly how the other associate botched the contract negotiations so badly. I'd given him everything he needed. Landing this client should have been a slam dunk."

"Obviously, your coworker doesn't have your level of skill," Megan said without a trace of sarcasm or irony. That was the other nice thing about family— even if they argued and teased, when the chips were down they had his back without question.

Right now he needed all the support he could get. He'd set his phone to silent when he and Grace went to bed last night and had woken this morning to a barrage of angry texts and messages from the firm's senior partner. Wiley had been leading a team over the last six months to land one of the biggest clients in their history. His extended stay in Texas had complicated the process, but he'd been diligent about conveying information to the associate who was the local point of contact in Chicago with their potential client. Much of Wiley's remote working had centered on this deal, which was set to close in two days. For some reason the client had pulled out without warning and no one at the firm could get a straight answer as to why.

He'd tried to convince his boss that he could handle the emergency from Texas, but the man gave him no choice. Hence, he was booked on a flight leaving early that afternoon.

Leaving today meant he'd miss Grace's preopening event, and he wanted to be there to watch her shine.

There had barely been time to say goodbye to her before he'd had to bolt from her apartment that morning, leaving her sleepy and rumpled in the bed. He couldn't believe how amazing it felt to finally make love to her, and he would have been happy to spend all weekend with her.

Wiley almost never spent extended periods of time with the women he dated, but as with everything, Grace broke the rules he'd set for relationships. He wanted her more for it.

He hadn't known when he'd left her that the work emergency was so dire that he'd be flying back to Chicago, and he wished he'd had time to call and explain it to her.

"I appreciate your vote of confidence," he said to his sister. "Just make sure to give my note to Grace, okay? I'm sure I'll talk to her before the reception, but I want her to have it."

Megan sat up on the bed and plucked the thin envelope from the nightstand. "I'd ask if you were with Grace last night, but she's staying at her parents', and I figure you've outgrown sneaking out of your girlfriends' windows so angry dads don't catch you."

He snorted. "Grace moved back to her apartment."

"Ah." Megan gave him a knowing smile.

"There's no 'ah,'" he muttered. "But I have to go. Just give her the note."

"I'll walk you out."

"No need."

"Sure there is." She followed him out of the room toward the front of the house. Everyone else was going about their daily business, so at least Wiley only had one sister to deal with. But one was more than enough. "You like Grace."

He tried to ignore the way his heart began to beat a staccato rhythm in his chest, telling him in no uncertain terms that he more than liked Grace.

"Everyone likes Grace. Don't you have some-where to be?"

"Not at the moment. It's okay to fall for a woman, Wiley. Especially one as sweet as Grace Williams. You were bound to find the right one at some point. I think it's wonderful that you've found her in Rambling Rose."

He'd just gotten to the front door but paused with his hand on the knob. "It's not wonderful. I'm leav-ing before her big event today, and I'm going back to Chicago for good once the hotel opens." He wasn't ready to reveal his meeting with Gavin. What if things didn't work out and he disappointed his sib-lings as well as Grace? He looked toward his sister, figuring her pained expression mirrored his. "Tell me how that's anything but the opposite of wonderful."

"Oh, Wi."

"Why?" he repeated, purposely misinterpreting her shortening of his name. "That's exactly what I'm wondering at the moment."

"You know Chicago isn't the only city that em-ploys attorneys," Megan told him, her voice gentle. "Even towns like Rambling Rose have need of them. You've done so much to help at the hotel so—"

"My time here is temporary." He walked out of the house and squinted against the bright light of morn-ing. "Grace and I both know it. Hell, it's what we agreed to in the first place. I'm not even sure she'd want me for longer."

"Don't be ridiculous. Women fall all over themselves for you. They always have."

He hit the button on the key fob to open the trunk. "Grace doesn't." He couldn't help the smile that tugged at his lips thinking about the way she didn't let him off the hook about anything. "She's stronger than people give her credit for," he said as he stowed the suitcase. It was the same thing he'd told Callum and Nicole, but he'd never get sick of saying it. "Independent, too. She's already told me she wants to focus on her career."

"Here's a pro tip." Megan placed a hand on his arm. "Women can have careers and successful relationships. Look at Stephanie and Ashley. Don't sell Grace short."

"I'm not." He opened the door to the car. "I just told you I thought she was strong."

"And don't use her strength and independence as an excuse."

Wiley shook his head. "Since when did my baby sisters grow up and get so smart?"

"We've always been smart." Megan rolled her eyes. "Me in particular."

"I've got to go. Give Grace the note and please tell her I'll be thinking of her. I'll call as soon as I can."

"Have a safe trip." She blew him a kiss. "We'll expect you back here as soon as you can make it."

* * *

Grace smiled as another coworker came up and congratulated her on the success of the local business owners' reception. There was no doubt she'd exceeded everyone's expectations. She gave partial credit to the beautiful weekend weather. It was unseasonably warm for the last weekend of January, even by Texas standards, with temperatures hovering in the low seventies and a cloudless blue sky above them. Although the trees planted around the hotel's pool held no leaves, they'd been strung with party lights, giving the impression of stars twinkling when they caught the sunlight.

The other businesses owned by the Fortunes had come out in force, from Stephanie giving information on local rescue animals to the spa staff doing five-minute chair massages and offering samples of the products they used with their clients.

There had been a steady stream of local business owners who'd meandered through the booths and demonstration tents that she'd had set up along the patio's perimeter. Jillian and Jay had done a great job with the photos of the hotel's interior they'd displayed on easels. According to Jay, they'd taken over two dozen reservations for the special local employee weekend Grace had arranged, and even more people had filled out tickets for the raffle to win a romantic dinner for two at Roja. Every business owner she'd invited had agreed to be part of their local partnership.

Grace had no doubt this gesture of good will would go a long way to encouraging Rambling Rose business owners to feel a sense of pride in the hotel once it opened, which would be key to making sure that out-of-town guests had an unforgettable experience during their stay in town.

She was also happy that no one had asked her specifically about the rumor of sabotage that had initially swirled around the balcony collapse. Grace did her best to reassure people that the accident hadn't been as bad as some wanted to believe and that she'd healed without any lingering issues.

The only thing that marred her happiness was that Wiley wasn't there with her. She'd received a voice message and text from him earlier explaining that the work emergency that had forced him to rush from her apartment early this morning had turned into something even bigger and he had to return to Chicago for a few days.

The timing couldn't have been worse, and not just because it meant he was missing today's preopening reception. Last night had been one of the most amazing in Grace's life. She'd felt so close to Wiley, like their connection would last beyond his stay in town. For him to leave the way he did… Well, she didn't want to read anything into it but couldn't seem to stop herself.

He'd seemed to enjoy himself as much as she had, but in truth Grace didn't really have the experience to judge that. Was their night together a onetime thing of finally being able to scratch an itch that had plagued them both? Or could it be more? Was it the start to the next step in their relationship that she desperately wanted?

"You don't look like someone who is basking in the glow of her success."

Grace turned to find her friend Collin standing next to her. "You came," she said, and reached out to hug him. "What do you think?"

He glanced around, lifting his sunglasses from his nose so she could see his dark gaze. "I think the Fortunes are lucky to have you working for them," he said. "Everyone I've talked to is suddenly huge fans of the hotel."

"Were people not fans before today?" The suggestion genuinely confused Grace. She thought the locals had overcome their concerns about the hotel when the Fortunes had changed plans based on community feedback.

"No one was talking too publicly about your accident," he said gently. "But it's a small town. People were still talking. I get the sense that the local business leaders now see that the hotel won't just be good for the Fortunes. The fact that you're here looking happy and toeing the Fortune line gives them a lot more confidence that everything's well with the construction."

"It is," she assured him. "They still don't exactly

know why the balcony collapsed. But from now on, it's going to be all good news coming from the hotel."

"Like you earning the general manager position," Collin said with a wink. "No one can hold a candle to the partnerships you're creating here, Grace."

Pride bloomed in her chest at her old friend's compliment. "Do you think so?" she asked, biting down on her lower lip. "I really want that job."

"You're going to get it." He nudged her shoulder. "I have a feeling about it."

She laughed. "Then I'm going to trust your feeling. We'll have to celebrate when you come back to town."

He crossed his arms over his broad chest. "I'm not sure your special Fortune friend would want you and me celebrating together. I could tell Wiley wasn't a fan of our friendship."

"That's not true," she argued, although she remembered Wiley's reaction to finding Collin sitting with her on her parents' porch. At the time, she'd been charmed by the fact that he might be jealous of her childhood friend. She'd wanted to believe it meant he didn't like the thought of her dating other men. Not that she and Collin were dating, but that wasn't outside the realm of possibility.

"So where is your new man?" Collin made a show of glancing around. "It seems like I can't trip without falling over a Fortune at this event, but I haven't seen Wiley."

"He's not my man," Grace clarified. "We're friends."

Collin lifted a brow. "Like you and I are friends?"

"Not exactly." She did her best not to squirm. "But he's not here. He had to fly back to Chicago for work."

"With no warning?"

"It was an emergency."

"Must have been important if he took off the morning of your moment in the spotlight."

"This partnership plan isn't about me," Grace said, forcing a neutral tone. She wasn't about to let anyone know that it hurt that Wiley wasn't here. "The point was to draw positive attention to the hotel. We did that. Joint effort."

"Grace." Collin gave her a gentle elbow jab. "We've been friends for a long time. You don't have to pretend with me."

She waved to Mariana and Jay, who were standing with Callum on the far side of the pool, then blew out a breath and turned to face Collin. "I'm upset that he had to leave, okay? Does that make you happy?"

"You know it doesn't."

"I'm sure it really was an emergency," she said, as much to convince herself as Collin. "He seemed worried about whatever was going on with his firm."

"But he didn't share details with you?"

"No," she admitted. "He called as he was getting on the airplane, but I missed it. His message didn't tell me much." She glanced up at the blue sky overhead, then checked her watch. "He's probably in the air right now."

"I hope he gets it worked out quickly. If not and he hurts you, I'll kick his butt."

"You'll have to get in line behind Jake," she said. "Please don't mention this to him. He still doesn't trust Wiley or the Fortunes, and I don't want to give him any more reason to be a jerk."

"Your brother isn't a jerk," Collin reminded her. "He cares about you. Just like I do."

"I know." Grace gave Collin a hug before he walked away.

She turned back to the crowd to see Nicole, Ashley and Megan watching her. Ashley and Megan waved, but Nicole's attention seemed to be focused on Collin's retreating back. Strange, Grace thought. She didn't think her friend knew the Fortune sisters, but she figured there were plenty of things going on that she wasn't aware of thanks to her own busy schedule.

Just as she was about to turn away, Megan called her name.

"Hey, Grace," the slender blonde said as she approached. "You've done such an amazing job today. Everyone's talking about the hotel but also about the spa and Provisions. It's like the other business owners finally see we want to work with them and they're willing to give us more of chance to prove it."

"That's great." Grace smiled again but this time

noticed how the muscles in her face were beginning to feel sore. Her leg ached, and her lower back was stiff from standing for so long today. She wondered if she'd feel so tired if she had Wiley at her side, then chided herself for even feeling a hint of depending on him. She'd learned that lesson with Craig. Grace knew she could only depend on herself. She had to be her own number one priority, not expect any man to make her his.

Even if Wiley had given every impression that he was doing exactly that.

"Are you okay?" Megan asked, concern obvious in her tone.

"Of course. I'm happy today has gone so well. I know the grand opening is going to be a huge success. Every business we invited today has agreed to be part of the downtown partnership so that should garner even more positive word of mouth for the hotel. You and your siblings have done so much for Rambling Rose. I'm honored to be a part of it."

"I know we're all glad to have you on the team." Megan pulled a thin envelope out of her purse. "I'm sorry but with all the excitement today, I forgot to give this to you." She handed the envelope to Grace, who was surprised to see her name scrawled across the front.

"It's from Wiley," Megan explained. "He felt bad about having to take off this morning. I know he wanted to be here for you today."

"Oh." Grace took the envelope and held it between two fingers. The urge to tear it open was strong, but she didn't want to read the note in front of Wiley's sister. Her emotions were jumbled at the moment, and she might reveal too much about her feelings for the missing Fortune.

"Don't worry." Megan patted Grace's arm. "I told him he has to come back to help with the last-minute grand opening preparations. He's not getting off easy with us. He can go back to his fancy big-city life when the work here is done."

Grace smiled, because that's what the other woman obviously expected, but inside her heart cracked. Megan had given her exactly the reminder she needed that even if Wiley returned, his time in Rambling Rose—and with Grace—was coming to an end.

And so were Grace's secret dreams for any possible future between them.

Chapter Fifteen

Two days later, Wiley popped the last bite of a stale turkey sandwich into his mouth and washed it down with a swig of cold coffee.

He glanced at the clock on his phone, not surprised to find that it was nearing midnight. He'd been working around-the-clock since he'd landed in Chicago on Saturday afternoon.

In almost a decade of practicing law, there had never been a deal that had gone so far south so quickly. The associate who was supposed to be managing the client while Wiley handled the bigger contract stipulations had wound up getting himself and their potential client's twenty-one-year-old son arrested in a gentleman's club Friday night. It had been a stupid, thoughtless rookie mistake, especially considering Ron Burnett, the company's CEO, had built his business on a motto of "family values." Now the entire deal was in jeopardy.

To make matters worse for Wiley, his boss had fired the associate, Jon Kirchman, after threatening to have him disbarred, and the young associate had taken every paper file he had regarding the contract with him and deleted all of the electronic correspondence and documents.

Wiley had spent the past twenty-four hours in constant contact with the firm's technology specialist in an attempt to recover the data. He'd reached out to Jon, hoping to convince him to turn over his files, but there had been no response yet.

Although no one specifically blamed Wiley for the crisis, he couldn't help but think that things wouldn't have gone so far off the rails if he hadn't been trying to manage the project remotely.

He'd never given less than 110 percent to his career but had to admit now that he'd returned to the office that the past few weeks in Rambling Rose had put that dedication to the test.

"Burning the late-night oil, I see."

Wiley stifled a yawn as Derek Curtis entered his office. Derek was a year older than Wiley, and they'd been hired with the firm at approximately the same time. Wiley respected the other man's instincts for negotiating contract transactions, although Derek had a tendency to start each week a bit slow on the uptake, often coming off a weekend of partying.

"We have a meeting with Ron Burnett and his board tomorrow. They're going to make the final vote on new corporate counsel." Wiley tapped a finger on one of the stacks of files that he and the paralegal staff had compiled. "I'm trying to make up a lot of ground from the hole Jon left us in."

"I still can't believe the guy just took off when he got fired. Who does that?"

Wiley shook his head. "Someone who isn't planning to have a law career in Chicago anytime soon."

"You need any help?" Derek lowered himself into the chair on the other side of Wiley's desk.

"I think I've done everything I can. I hope it's enough."

"This isn't your fault," Derek reminded him.

"Why does it feel that way? If I'd been here to head up the deal instead of trying to manage it from Texas…"

"Tell me about Texas." Derek sat forward. "You never explained exactly why you extended your stay. When we talked before you headed down there, you were planning on doing the family duty stuff, then heading back as soon as possible."

"It ended up being important for me to help with a few things at my family's hotel."

"A few things? Legal issues?"

Wiley shrugged. He didn't really want to share details of his life in Texas. It felt so separate from his life in the city, and he had no doubt his coworker and sometime-friend wouldn't understand the appeal. "A construction accident."

"Was anyone hurt?"

"One of the employees broke her ankle."

"Ouch." Derek whistled under his breath. "Sounds like a workers' comp lawsuit waiting to happen. You're making sure to cover your a—"

"Grace isn't going to sue the hotel," he said through clenched teeth.

"How do you know?" Derek shook his head. "I once saw a guy trip over his own two feet on a building site and then sue for six figures."

"I know her," Wiley said, then immediately regretted the words based on the smile Derek gave him.

"Is that so? Smart move, Counselor."

"It's not like that. We're friends."

Derek chuckled. "I get it."

"No, you don't." Wiley couldn't decide whether the exhaustion of working so many hours or the stress of the deal or simply missing Grace so badly was making him want to stand up and punch his colleague in the face. Maybe a combination of all those things.

"Come on, don't get bent out of shape," Derek said. "I've heard how you talk about your family, even if you don't see them a lot. We both know you're going to protect blood over some piece of—"

"Stop talking." Wiley pushed back from his desk. "Grace isn't going to come after the hotel, and I'm not friends with her for any other reason than I like spending time with her."

"But it's not serious, right?" Derek leaned back in his chair, and Wiley had the secret wish that he'd topple backward. "I know you, Wiley. You don't do serious. We're the same. Relationships are a distraction and never worth the trouble. You know that."

Wiley stared at the other attorney.

Derek gestured to the papers piled all over the desk. "If nothing else, the situation you're in now proves it. The reason you stayed in Texas was a chick, and look at what it's led to. You could lose everything you've worked for over one deal that wasn't managed right."

"I'm not going to lose anything," Wiley said, although he knew Derek was right. Wiley had taken his eye off the ball, and now he was struggling to make sure he kept it in the air.

"Let me know if you need help," Derek offered again as he rose from the chair. "My focus is right where it needs to be. Always."

"Thanks," Wiley muttered, then sank back down in his chair as the other man disappeared into the hall. He shut down his computer and began to pack up his briefcase. The rest of what needed to be reviewed before tomorrow could be handled in the morning. Right now, he needed a few hours of rest to get his head on straight again.

He didn't want to admit that Grace had been the reason he'd prolonged his stay in Rambling Rose or that his preoccupation with her had affected his work. He'd continued to manage his clients and his job from the tiny Texas town. More importantly, he'd been able to reconnect with his brothers and sisters. That was worth more than anything else.

Although perhaps not more than the career he'd dedicated the last ten years of his life to.

He had to keep focused now. Get through tomorrow and land the client, then he could think about what came next. He was supposed to meet with the senior partners at his cousin's firm in Austin in a couple of days, but Wiley wasn't even sure what he wanted now. Could he really close the biggest deal of his life and then walk away to start over halfway across the country?

His brother and sisters had made it work, but he'd always been different. The odd Fortune out, so to speak. What would happen if he tried to start over?

What would happen if he told Grace the truth about his feelings for her?

As he flipped off the light to his office, his phone buzzed with an incoming text. A message from Grace. Simple, to the point, and the words utterly gutted him.

I miss you.

How could one simple sentence possibly convey so much?

His heart seemed to skip a beat as he ran a thumb over the smooth screen, as if he could somehow reach out and touch her across the miles.

He gave his head a hard shake and pocketed the phone. As much as he wanted to respond or to call her, he'd promised himself that his focus would remain on work until he salvaged the deal with Ron and his company. The firm was counting on him, and he already felt as if he'd let them down.

Grace knew how he felt about her. She would wait. He had to take care of his current life if he was going to truly choose a future with her.

"I think we're nearly there," Nicole announced as she placed plates filled with roasted chicken and Brie over pasta on the table in front of Grace, Jillian and Jay.

"Everything we make is delicious," Mariana said with a genuine smile as she poured sparkling lemonade into their glasses.

"Some of the best food I've ever eaten." Jay scooped another huge bite of chicken into his mouth. "Seriously the best."

"Not that you probably have much to compare it

to," Jillian said with a delicate sniff. "I've actually traveled to both London and Paris."

Jay gave a haughty sniff. "Well, la-di-da then," he said, his Southern accent especially thick.

Grace pressed a napkin to her mouth to hide her giggle. "I'm certain Jay has a very discriminating palate," she said, wanting to be loyal to her friend in the face of Jillian's snobbery.

"Very," he agreed with mock severity, then winked at Grace.

She grinned and took a bite of the pasta, which truly was delicious. Mariana and Nicole discussed the dish as a potential winter season special while the three trainees enjoyed their lunch.

Nicole was continuing to refine the Roja menu with the grand opening around the corner. Her attention to detail and understanding of how to meld flavors together to showcase a variety of refined but still comforting foods amazed Grace. She had no doubt that the restaurant was going to be a huge success and bolster the hotel's reputation.

Jillian and Jay continued to banter back and forth. It amused Grace to no end how much Jay seemed to enjoy irritating their uptight coworker. He might joke about his country roots while Jillian took great pleasure in giving him grief over his lack of worldliness, but there was something more to Jay Cross. Beyond his easygoing manner, Grace sensed a depth of experience he didn't want to share, so she never pushed him to reveal what had led him to Rambling Rose in the first place.

She understood the desire to make a fresh start without the past coloring every step.

Something caught her attention, and she turned in her seat to see Wiley entering the restaurant. He'd been gone almost a week. In that short time her emotions had run the gamut from disappointment to anger to heartbreak to resignation. Grace wanted to believe she'd settled on acceptance, especially when they'd barely spoken on the phone and he'd only sent a few short texts that told her no details of the emergency that forced him to leave so suddenly and when he would return.

Her brain might have taken the hint about him walking—or literally running—away the morning after making love to her, but her body hadn't gotten the message. Not when he looked as handsome as ever in a dark sweater and jeans with cowboy boots that finally appeared to be broken in. Like he belonged in Texas and in her world, although his absence this week had told her that wasn't true.

Grace had been thrown back into the same emotional turmoil she'd felt after her breakup with Craig. Of course it was different with Wiley, because he hadn't cheated on her or made her any promises about the future. Somehow that only made her heart hurt more.

She'd told herself after returning to town that she

was going to focus on herself and not let anything distract her from her goals. Instead, she'd spent the past few days making excuses to go to the bathroom at the hotel and fight back tears. Everything about her daily life reminded her of Wiley. The way she'd looked forward to seeing him in the hall, to stealing kisses in the office and to spending her evenings in his arms.

The Hotel Fortune had been her chance at a brand-new life, but she couldn't even walk into the lobby without thinking of Wiley. It had gotten so bad that she'd actually considered quitting her job and leaving Rambling Rose to reinvent herself again in a place that held no emotional pull for her.

It had been Collin who'd talked her off that ledge, reminding her that this was her home and she belonged here as much as any member of the Fortune family. Everything had made sense when Wiley wasn't nearby, but watching him walk toward the table, his gaze intense on her, her thoughts and feelings scattered like dandelion fluff in a strong wind.

"You're back," Nicole called to her brother as she turned.

Grace hated the jealousy that stabbed at her heart when Nicole gave him a huge hug. Grace yearned to touch him, but she had no right. They'd agreed to date secretly—her plan—but it hadn't been nearly enough. She wanted more. More than she should and likely more than Wiley was capable of giving her. It was time to remember that.

"Something smells amazing," he said.

"Your sister has outdone herself with this dish." Mariana came to stand next to Jay's chair. "We have three discerning customers right here." She patted Jay's shoulder. "If an empty plate is any indication, Roja is ready for business."

"I have no doubt," Wiley said, offering his sister a proud smile. "Any chance you have leftovers? I haven't had a decent meal in what feels like days. I've been living off takeout the entire trip."

Grace tamped down her sympathy. Now that she looked at him more closely, she could see the lines of exhaustion fanning out from his dark eyes and bracketing his mouth. It only made her want to pull him to her and offer whatever comfort she could.

Stupid, she reminded herself. She wasn't a love-sick schoolgirl anymore. The man had made it clear where his priorities were, and she needed to do the same.

As if reading her thoughts, Nicole pushed away and wagged a finger in front of Wiley. "I shouldn't give you even a bite. I forgot that I'm mad at you. You practically ghosted us this week. We didn't even know if you were coming back before the opening."

"Of course I was coming back." He looked genuinely surprised. "I told you I'd be here to help."

"Give your brother a break," Mariana said with a

gentle tsk. "He's here now." Her knowing gaze met Grace's across the table. "When the three of you are finished here, I'd love to get your thoughts on some of the grand opening events."

Grace pushed back from the table. "I actually have a meeting scheduled with Ellie to finalize plans to put a link for the hotel on the town's website."

"Smart plan." Nicole gave her an enthusiastic thumbs-up.

Jillian's lips pursed but she didn't say anything or try to one-up Grace, which made Grace suspicious. "Jay and I can take care of whatever Mariana needs," Jillian offered, then rolled her eyes when Grace gave her a shocked look.

Grace could feel Wiley's gaze on her but purposely didn't make eye contact with him. If Jillian was being nice enough to give her an out, Grace must not be doing as good a job at hiding her feelings as she hoped.

She thanked Nicole and Mariana for lunch, then hurried from the restaurant and out the hotel's front entrance, not even bothering to grab her purse from the office. She needed fresh air and a few minutes to gather her thoughts.

Wiley was back. She shouldn't be surprised. He had told her—and clearly his siblings—that he planned to return before the opening.

She just wished she could turn off her feelings for him as easily as he seemed to be able to manage it.

The afternoon was cloudy, and a brisk breeze whipped down the town's main street, making her regret the choice to rush out without a jacket. At least the cool air felt good on her heated skin.

"Grace."

Her stomach pitched and tumbled at the sound of Wiley's voice behind her. She turned, forcing a bland smile on her face as he jogged toward her.

"Hi," he said, and lifted his hand as if to reach for her but then lowered it again. He searched her face as if he couldn't quite understand why she wasn't greeting him with more enthusiasm, but Grace had finally gotten her body and heart under control, even though it felt like it was shattering inside her chest.

"How was your trip home?" She crossed her arms over her chest.

"Home," he repeated with a frown. "You mean back to Chicago?"

"Your home," she said, nodding. "I hope it was productive."

"We closed the deal. The firm is now the counsel for the largest plexiglass manufacturer in the US."

"Congratulations." Grace made a show of checking her watch. "I need to go. I don't want to be late for my appointment with Ellie."

"I'll walk with you," he offered.

"No."

His frown deepened. "What's wrong, Grace? Is

it your leg? Are you doing too much? If you need a break, I can talk to—"

She held up a hand, hating that her body responded to his offer of support. Hating that she didn't trust that he wasn't being kind to make certain she didn't cause trouble for his family. As much as she wanted to deny Jake's suspicions about Wiley's motives, his lack of communication had made her doubt everything she felt for him.

"I don't need you to talk to anyone on my behalf. I can manage my life and my career on my own, Wiley. I've been handling things just fine without you here."

"I know you can manage on your own," he said gently. "But I want to help, Grace. I care about you."

"Right." She bit off the word and forced her voice not to tremble. "We're friends."

"More than friends."

"Friends," she repeated, because if she allowed herself to entertain the thought of more, she'd be a goner for sure. "That's all."

"I don't understand. I missed you, Grace. Every moment away from you was—"

"Don't." *Don't say sweet things. Don't look at me with confusion and pain in your eyes.*

She swallowed, knowing she needed to be able to mutter more than one-syllable words at him. She needed to end this. The torture of being so close and yet feeling so far away from what she wanted her life to be. "I had some time to think about the future while you were gone, Wiley. I wasn't distracted by—" she waved a hand in his general direction "—by anything. The truth is we agreed what was between us would be temporary, and it's better that it end sooner rather than later."

A muscle jumped in jaw. "Better for whom?"

"Me," she whispered. "Both of us, I'm guessing, but I have to think about myself and my future. I can't... I won't put you ahead of me. Do you understand that?"

He shook his head. "I don't understand anything apparently."

"We're friends," she repeated. "That's all we were ever meant to be."

He stared at her long and hard like he wanted to argue. A piece of her wanted him to argue. She wanted him to fight for her, but she should have known better. Grace wasn't the type of woman that men fought for. She was a woman who fit herself into the compartment the people in her life needed her to be in.

But no more.

"Welcome back, Wiley. I'm sure your brothers and sisters will be thrilled to have you here again."

Without waiting for his response, she turned and walked away.

Chapter Sixteen

"I'm mad at you."

Wiley continued to stare at the basketball game playing on the television of the sitting room in his suite at the ranch, ignoring his sister's arrival.

"Really mad," Nicole said, walking into the room and picking up the remote from the side table. She pushed a button, and the TV went dark.

"Big brothers are supposed to make sisters mad," Wiley said. "It's part of the job description."

"Do you want to know why?" She sat on the chair next to the sofa.

"Not really." He took a long pull on the beer he'd been nursing for the past hour. "You know I was watching that game?"

"What was the score?" she demanded.

He shrugged. "One of the teams was winning."

Nicole's mouth curved into a smile. "Yeah, you were real invested in the game, Wi. Seriously, we need to talk."

"Not in the mood," he told her. Since Grace had basically broken off their temporary relationship in the middle of the street two days ago, Wiley hadn't been in the mood for anything. He'd kept himself busy and tried not to think about Grace, which was virtually impossible, especially when she seemed to be involved in almost every last-minute detail of the hotel's grand opening.

He'd found himself following her scent through an upstairs hallway yesterday until he'd heard her voice in one of the guest rooms, discussing something with Jillian and Jay. Wiley had ducked into a housekeeping closet when they came out to avoid being spotted. As he stared at shelves filled with crisp white linens and tiny bottles of toiletries, he'd realized how bad off he was with missing her.

Unlike him, Grace didn't seem the least bit affected by their breakup, if that's what he could call it. She appeared completely focused on making sure the grand opening went off without a hitch. Despite his heartache, he was so proud of her for the leadership role she'd taken on and the way her confidence had bloomed. He only wished he could share in the success with her.

"What did you do to Grace?"

Wiley sucked in a breath as he straightened. "Nothing. Not one damn thing, Nicole."

"It's obvious she's hurting."

"Not to me," he countered.

"Then you're a bigger fool than I suspected. Even Jillian is being nice, so you know Grace must be really upset. I thought you liked her."

"I did. I do."

"Then why dump her, Wiley? Especially right before the opening. I understand that commitment isn't your thing and being back in Chicago probably had you missing the city, but—"

"You have it wrong." He pointed the tip of his bottle toward his sister. "I was the dumpee in this situation. Grace broke up with me."

"Impossible," Nicole said immediately. "Women don't break up with you."

"I guess there's a first time for everything."

"What did you do?"

He placed the beer bottle on the coffee table with distinct thud. "Nothing."

His sister's blue eyes narrowed. "Are you sure?"

"How could I have done anything?" He lifted his hands, palms up, and didn't bother to hide his frustration. "I was working around-the-clock in Chicago to salvage the deal. There was no time for anything, not that I would have wanted it, anyway. I missed her."

"Did you tell her that?"

He nodded. "Right in front of the hotel when I got back. Just before she cut me off at the knees."

"And she gave no indication of being unhappy while you were away?"

"I don't know, Nicole. I was away. Maybe her brother convinced her not to trust me. Maybe she realized she doesn't want to deal with the complications of our family."

"Grace isn't the type to shy away from things that are hard," Nicole reminded him. "In fact, we all keep forgetting she's wearing the boot, because she doesn't let it slow her down one bit."

"She's amazing," he murmured. "Probably too smart to want something long-term with me."

"I don't believe that." Nicole tapped a finger against her chin. "You two were the worst-kept secret in town. Everyone could see she was crazy about you. Did she say anything when you talked to her during your trip that would give you a clue—"

"We didn't talk while I was gone."

Nicole's mouth dropped open. "You were in Chicago for nearly a week."

"I'm aware."

"How could you not talk to her?"

He shrugged. "It wasn't purposeful. I was busy."

"Not an excuse."

Agitation rolled through Wiley like a tidal wave. He didn't want to think that he was at fault. How could that be? No, he hadn't told Grace how he felt before he left. But she had to know, or at least have an idea. He'd never devoted so much of himself to a woman before. In fact, it had scared the hell out of him, especially when he returned to Chicago and saw the mess his firm had almost ended up in because he'd been distracted by his family and Grace while in Texas. Guilt had eaten at him, which was part of the reason he hadn't done the best job of communicating while he was away. But still...

He stood from the sofa and paced to the edge of the room. No way would he believe that he was the reason she'd broken things off. That simply couldn't be the case.

"I did call, Nicole. Or I tried." He heard the edge in his voice but regaining control was the last thing on his mind. He had to understand why she'd ended things between them. He had to know if there was a chance at winning her back. "We had trouble connecting because of how much I was at the office. It wasn't like I slept with her and then took off without a backward glance." He cringed when Nicole sucked in a harsh gasp, realizing exactly what he'd just blurted. Wiley would give anything if he could take the last ten seconds back.

"You slept with her?" Nicole moved to the edge of the seat, looking like their mother used to when she wanted to throttle one of the boys for making a stupid mistake.

"Forget I said anything." He shook his head. "I'm not thinking clearly, obviously. I shouldn't have—"

"She's our employee," Nicole reminded him through clenched teeth.

"Yours," Wiley countered. "Not mine. My relationship with her has nothing to do with the hotel."

"Does she know that?"

He opened his mouth to answer then shut it again.

Nicole's eyes widened. "Did she tell you about her ex-boyfriend?"

"The one who cheated on her?" Wiley nodded. "That has nothing to do with me, either."

"How much did she share about their breakup?"

"She didn't need to explain much. He cheated. End of story."

"Wiley."

"Stop sounding like Mom," he told her. "Your tone is freaking me out."

"I did Grace's reference check at Cowboy Country," Nicole said quietly. "The story she gave me about how things ended there was a little convoluted. I spoke with her boss in Horseback Hollow. Grace was an exemplary employee, just like she is for us. But when she discovered that her boyfriend was cheating on her with another coworker, there was a bit of a scene."

"What kind of a scene?" Wiley asked, even though he wasn't sure he wanted to know the answer.

"I only heard the details because the amusement

park manager felt bad for Grace and wanted her to get the position in the training program. Apparently, the whole thing blew up at an employee picnic. The ex very loudly blamed Grace. He made it known that he was cheating because Grace lacked—" she made a face "—spark in the bedroom."

Wiley breathed out a string of curses that would have horrified his mother. "She doesn't lack spark. Grace is the sparkliest damn woman I've ever known."

"Too much information." Nicole stood, making a show of covering her ears. "I don't want to talk about you and Grace and sparks. But think of the timing, Wi. The two of you…" She shrugged. "Took things to the next level and then you left town and didn't call her."

"I called. We just didn't get to talk." He cursed again because he hated knowing that he'd made Grace doubt anything about herself. Making love to her had been the most wonderful time of his life. Not that he had any intention of discussing details with his sister.

"Maybe you should try talking to her again," Nicole suggested gently. "If you really care about her."

"I care." He ran a hand through his hair. "I more than care about her."

"You can say the word." Nicole crossed to him and patted his arm. "It won't burn your tongue to speak it out loud."

"It might," he muttered, then sighed. "I love her, Nicole. I'm *in* love with her. I didn't expect it, and I'm not sure I want it."

His sister squealed with delight. "I knew it. We all knew it. Ashley, Megan and I knew it before you did. We're so much smarter than you."

He pulled away, although he couldn't help the way his mouth curved. "Why do you all have to keep pointing it out? I should mention it's annoying. If you're finished gloating, can we talk about how I'm going to fix this?"

"Do you *want* to fix it?"

He thought about it for a long moment. Although he expected panic to rise up inside him, instead he felt a sense of peace settle in his chest. "Yes."

She inclined her head. "Why do I think there's a 'but' coming?"

"More like an 'and,'" he admitted. "I need to figure some things out. I haven't done a great job of making her feel like she's a priority for me, and Grace deserves that. I want to give her that, Nic. I don't want to mess it up."

"What if Grace says no? Will you go back to Chicago?"

He shook his head. "My time in the city is finished. No matter what happens with Grace, I'm moving to Texas. Our big, crazy family used to feel like something I needed to escape. It didn't feel like I could have my own life when I was just one of the Fortune brothers."

"You've always been more than that," his sister said quietly.

"Took me a bit of time to realize it." He grinned at her. "It really grates on my nerves that my baby sisters are so smart, but you're right. I've had a great life in Chicago, but it's never been home. Home is where family is, and I want to put down roots in Texas. I want this place to be my home."

Grace climbed the stairs leading to Roja's banquet room on Tuesday morning, trying hard to control the nerves fluttering through her chest.

Callum had texted her last night, asking her to arrive at the hotel early the following morning for a private meeting. With less than a week until the grand opening, she couldn't imagine why the head of Fortune Brothers Construction would want to take time out of his busy schedule to meet with her, unless he'd found out about her relationship with Wiley.

After their breakup, Grace had done her best to go back to business as usual at work. It wasn't easy, because her body and her heart seemed tuned in to his presence like a radio dial. If he was anywhere nearby, awareness shivered across her skin, and it was difficult to draw a steady breath.

Yesterday she'd overheard Nicole tell Mariana that Wiley had gone to Austin for business. Of course, it was silly for Grace to be disappointed that he hadn't said goodbye to her. She'd told him she just wanted to be friends, but they both knew they couldn't go back to simple friendship after what they'd shared.

She'd walked away before she was tempted to ask Nicole how long he'd be gone and what his plans for the future were. Anything Grace heard was bound to hurt, since she understood his future wouldn't involve her.

The timing of this meeting seemed a bit of a coincidence, and part of her feared that the Fortunes would blame her for Wiley leaving again. She knew he would never try to put her in a bad position or do anything that might jeopardize her job, but after the way things ended in Horseback Hollow, it was difficult for her to trust that. She'd thought her future at Cowboy Country was secure until Craig had publicly humiliated her.

Her anxiety went into overdrive when she turned to find Callum seated at a banquet table along with Nicole and Kane. It felt like Grace was facing the Fortune tribunal.

"Good morning," she said, clearing her throat when the words came out sounding like a croak.

"Hey, Grace." Callum and his cousin stood as she approached. "How are you doing?" Callum glanced at her leg. "Damn, I'm sorry. I figured there'd be more privacy up here, but we probably should have met downstairs. I keep forgetting about your injury."

"It's fine," Grace assured him. "The walking boot makes it relatively easy to get around, and I'm slow on steps, but I can manage."

"Of course you can," Kane agreed with a chuckle. "These past few weeks have proven that you can manage just about anything."

Except holding on to Wiley, she thought to herself. "Thanks," she answered Kane. "What can I do for all of you today?"

Nicole offered a kind smile and gestured to the seat across from them. "Let's talk for a few minutes."

Grace's heart sank, and she wanted to run in the other direction. That's exactly how the conversation with her bosses at the amusement park had begun, during which it had become painfully obvious that the best course of action for everyone would be her resignation.

She did not want to give up her future at the hotel. An image of Wiley flashed in her mind. Would she walk away from the Fortunes if it meant another chance with him? Probably, although that might make her a fool. She'd never felt anything like she did when she was with Wiley. Regret made her chest pinch, and she wondered for the millionth time if she'd given up on him too easily.

Slipping into the chair, she kept her hands clasped tightly in front of her. "Is there a problem with last-minute details for the opening?"

Nicole shook her head. "Everything is right on

schedule. You, Jillian and Jay have done an incredible job."

"Far surpassed our expectations," Callum added.

"I'm glad." Grace forced a smile. "So what I am doing here?"

"The plan had been to choose the employee who would be promoted to the general manager position after the grand opening," Nicole explained. "It made sense to get through this last push and then focus on the future."

Grace nodded.

"But recent events have made us rethink the timing of our announcement." Callum inclined his head. "We want to show stability, to make sure that people understand we have things well under control at the Hotel Fortune."

"We're moving forward and expecting nothing but good things." Kane glanced behind him at the doors that led to the balcony.

The balcony that had collapsed with Grace on it.

"Okay." Grace's cheeks started to throb as she tried to keep her smile in place. Recent events? They had to be talking about her accident, and it felt as though her fall from the second floor was a metaphor for her life. Just when she thought she had time to pause and enjoy the view, she went tumbling off the edge. She should have known this would happen. Of course they wouldn't choose her for the general manager position. She was the physical representation of a public relations nightmare. The Fortunes would be smart to promote someone who was untarnished by any scandal. Jillian fit that bill without—

"What do you think, Grace?"

She blinked as Callum leaned forward, giving her an odd look, and she tried to catch up with the thread of the conversation.

"I think it's a wise decision."

His mouth twitched. "Then you're accepting the position?"

She blinked. "I think I missed something."

Nicole laughed. "He just offered you the general manager job."

"Oh." Grace sucked in a shallow breath. "I thought you were telling me I wasn't a fit because of the accident. I'm bad PR."

"On the contrary," Callum told her. "You've done more to bolster the hotel's image in town than we could have imagined. The partnership with the local businesses is going to be integral to our reputation as we open."

"Thank you," she whispered. "I'd be honored to accept the promotion. But…" She bit down on the inside of her cheek as she tried to determine the best way to share this next bit.

Kane sighed. "I hate a 'but.'"

"What is it?" Nicole asked gently, placing her hand on her cousin's beefy arm.

"I'm in love with your brother," she said, and Kane choked on the sip of water he'd just taken.

"Which one?"

"She's talking about our brother," Nicole clarified. "Wiley. You love Wiley."

"Yes." Grace nodded. "But we broke up."

Callum's mouth dropped open. "You were dating Wiley?"

"Get with the program," Nicole said, swatting his arm.

"What did he do?" Kane demanded. "Do I need to kill him?"

Grace almost laughed at the absurdity of that statement. "No, of course not. He didn't do anything. I just chose… My priority is the hotel. I want you to know that. I don't want there to be any doubts."

"You can have both," Callum said, as if it were the simplest thing in the world.

Grace squeezed her eyes shut for a moment, then opened them again. She could be the biggest idiot in the world for revealing all of this in a meeting where she was being offered her dream job. "That hasn't worked so well for me in the past."

"Wiley isn't him," Nicole told her with so much understanding that it felt like Grace's heart might break all over again.

"Who?" Kane and Callum asked in unison.

"I know." Grace kept her gaze focused on Wiley's sister. "I just wanted you to know where things stood.

It's meant a lot to Wiley to reconnect with all of you. As much as I'm looking forward to a long career at the hotel, it won't be at the expense of his relationship with his family."

Nicole leaned forward. "Are you saying you'd give up the promotion if he wasn't comfortable with you working here?"

Was that what Grace was telling them? How was that possible? The general manager job was everything she'd wanted for her life and a vindication of what she'd been through in Horseback Hollow. Wiley hadn't given her the impression that he wanted her to forgo her dream for him. Not once. He'd only been supportive and proud as she dedicated herself to her job.

But she knew how important his family was and understood the toll that feeling distanced from them had taken on him. She wouldn't be a part of that.

"Yes." The pain she expected at saying the word didn't materialize. Instead, she felt as if her world had stopped spinning and righted itself in a way that put her exactly where she wanted to be.

"That's ridiculous." Callum shook his head. "Wiley is a grown damn man. You're important to the hotel. To our family. He'll deal."

"But if not—"

"Thank you, Grace," Nicole said. "You've proven even more why you're the right person for this job.

We appreciate your loyalty and look forward to many years of you being part of Team Fortune."

"Really?" Grace swallowed. "I mean, that's what I want, as well." She pushed back from the table. "Just know that I have the best interests of the hotel at the forefront of my mind. Always."

"We know." Nicole stood and then came around the table to hug her. "And we appreciate it. We'll talk to Jillian and Jay as well and then plan to make the big announcement to the staff. Congratulations."

Chapter Seventeen

"Oh, hell, no."

"Hi, Jake." Wiley stepped out onto the path in front of Grace's brother, ignoring his less-than-cordial greeting. "Mind if I join you?"

Jake didn't break stride as he ran past Wiley on the dirt trail that wound through one of the local parks. "If you can keep up, Wyatt."

Wiley also didn't correct the mistake of his name. He simply ran alongside the other man, grateful for his almost-daily runs along Lake Michigan when he'd lived in Chicago. Jake set one hell of a pace.

They did a fast loop around the park's perimeter, passing a few families and slower joggers. The exercise actually helped to clear Wiley's jumbled thoughts. He was clear about what he wanted, but how to convince Grace's recalcitrant brother that his intentions were honorable was another story.

"We need to talk about your sister," Wiley said, huffing for breath, as they approached the parking lot where the trail ended.

"You hurt her," Jake said, and then bent at the waist. At least Wiley wasn't the only one sucking wind, a small consolation when it felt as though his lungs were on fire.

"I want to make it right. I love her."

Jake glanced up at him, a sneer curling one side of his mouth. "You don't have to say that. She's not going to come after your precious family and the hotel. Even if they wouldn't have handed her the promotion she—"

"Grace earning the general manager position had nothing to do with her injury." Wiley placed his hands on his hips and drew in big gulps of air, struggling to keep the temper out of his voice. He was here to win Jake over to his side, not to antagonize him further. But Wiley couldn't tolerate the suggestion that Grace had been offered the manager role at the hotel for any other reason than she deserved it.

"I know she's qualified," her brother conceded. "But even you have to admit—"

"I don't have to admit anything. Grace worked her butt off, both before and after the accident. She's a huge asset to the hotel, and everyone in my family sees that. We're not the ones selling her short."

Jake straightened. "What's that supposed to mean?"

"Why are you so hell-bent on convincing her that she can't make it on her own?"

"I'm not—"

"How do you think it makes her feel when her family is constantly telling her that the reason she's being recognized has more to do with her injury than her talent and skills?" For the moment, Wiley put aside trying to smooth the waters with Grace's brother. He couldn't stand to listen to one more suggestion that she was anything less than fully capable on her own.

"We don't do that."

"Are you sure? Because that's how it sounds to me. I fell in love with your sister and not because I was trying to protect my family or any other sort of cheap attorney tricks you might want to accuse me of. The fact is she's the most amazing woman I know. She's smart, strong and creative. She doesn't give up or give in, and we both know how big her heart is. She'd do anything for the people she loves."

Jake stared at him for several long moments, then looked away. "Did your brother or sister mention that Grace told them she wouldn't take the promotion if it upset you to have her at the hotel?"

"Yeah." Wiley kicked a small rock with the toe of

one sneaker, sending it skittering across the grass. "I would never let that happen, and neither would they. I want another chance with Grace, but it's her choice. If she's truly moved on from me, I'll respect the decision. Her place at the hotel is secure, and my brothers and sisters would never treat her unfairly."

"I know."

"In fact—" Wiley broke off as he tried to digest those two words coming from Jake. He was ready to argue as long as he needed to in order to convince her brother that his family had Grace's interests at heart. "You know what?"

"I'm not fully sold on the Fortunes," Jake said, wiping a sleeve across his forehead. "Trusting people outside my close circle of friends and family...well, it's been a struggle since the accident. Grace gave up a lot to come home and help during my recovery."

"She told me about that time," Wiley said. "I know she was happy to have the chance to pitch in and remains grateful that everything turned out okay for you."

"She's the best." Jake flashed a rueful smile. "We can agree on that."

"Yeah."

"And even though you aren't the man I'd choose for her, you're the one she's chosen."

Wiley mulled that over for a few seconds, then chuckled. "I can't decide if that's a compliment or an insult."

Jake's grin widened. "We'll call it a compliment. My sister deserves to be happy more than any person I know. If you make her happy, that's good enough for me."

"I appreciate that, Jake." Wiley held out a hand, and the other man shook it. "Family is important to Grace and to me. I want us to get along. You can believe me when I tell you I'll do my best to make her happy every day if she gives me another chance."

"I believe you, Fortune." Jake nodded. "You should know that if you ever hurt her, I'll be there."

Wiley shook his head. "Don't worry about that. You'll have to get in line behind most of my siblings. But all of this is moot if I can't convince her to try again. To be honest, I've never had to work very hard with women. That's another thing I love about your sister. She makes me want to try."

"What you need is a plan," Jake said, clapping Wiley on the shoulder as they headed toward their cars. "Grace is used to being the one to put in the effort. I think your willingness to try will go a long way."

"I hope it goes far enough," Wiley murmured, then stopped walking as an idea popped into his head. He turned to face Grace's brother, an unexpected ally but the perfect one for what Wiley wanted to accomplish. "And I hope that you'll help me make sure it does."

* * *

"Jake, are you sure we can't just get him something from the hardware store in town?" Grace drummed her fingers against her jeans and tried not to sound as impatient as she felt. Her brother had asked her to drive with him to pick up a gift for their dad's upcoming birthday.

Even though Grace had what felt like a never-ending to-do list with the opening in a few days, she'd agreed to accompany Jake on his errand. She and her brother hadn't been on the best terms lately, and she didn't want any more animosity between them.

Unfortunately, Jake hadn't mentioned that the place he was picking up some vintage baseball glove for Dad was a good half hour out of town. He'd been in a strange mood since picking her up at her apartment, uncharacteristically peppy one minute and then anxious the next.

"It's important, Gracie," he said, and gave her a bright smile. Way too bright for her to believe it was sincere. "This is going to be the best surprise ever."

"You're acting weird," she said as she looked out the window of his truck. The last time she'd driven this stretch of highway had been with Wiley on their first date.

A dull ache filled her chest at the thought of Wiley Fortune. The past few days without him had been awful. Grace missed him like crazy, even though she saw him around the hotel almost every day. But it wasn't the same.

Jillian and Jay had taken her out for a drink to celebrate her promotion. It astounded Grace that Jillian seemed to accept the decision the Fortunes had made without complaint. Grace realized that she had Jillian to thank, in part, for the opportunity. Their rivalry had pushed Grace outside her comfort zone and motivated her to go the extra mile with every task she was assigned.

Obviously, it had paid off, but the price for her success was steep. Grace wondered if she should have given Wiley more of a chance after he returned from Chicago. She'd been hurt and felt rejected because he hadn't called while away, but part of her knew she was transferring her emotions about her last relationship onto this one. Her ex's betrayal made her so sensitive to any slight. She'd built giant walls around her heart because that had seemed like the best way to protect it.

She was coming to understand that keeping potential hurt out almost meant that the love she had to give someone was trapped inside her. Yet as much as she wanted to risk her heart for Wiley, it was difficult to imagine how much it might shatter if he didn't want to try again.

She'd told herself she would wait until after the grand opening celebration and then reach out to him.

That way she'd have the time to fall apart in a way she didn't at the moment.

"You're so quiet," Jake said as he pulled into the right-hand lane of the highway and turned on his signal to exit. "Are you tired?"

"I'm fine." She leaned forward in her seat. "Where are you going? Why are you getting off here?"

"It's our exit." He gave her a sidelong glance. "What's wrong?"

"Nothing," she lied. It was the exit for the Oak Tree Inn. As Jake turned at the end of the ramp, she realized they were going to drive right past the converted farmhouse on the way to wherever this special baseball glove was located. It shouldn't bother her to see the place that she and Wiley had shared their first kiss. She'd handled much more challenging situations than a simple driveway. So why was her heart practically beating out of her chest?

"I want you to be happy, Grace." Jake's voice held a note of tenderness she wasn't used to hearing from her tough brother. "You deserve that."

"We both do," she answered.

"Wiley made you happy."

Her mouth dropped open at those words. "I don't want another lecture about the Fortunes, especially Wiley."

"It was an observation," he countered. "Not a lecture."

She smiled despite the sadness coursing through her. "I figured the lecture was coming next."

"You have no idea what's coming next," Jake said softly, and then shocked Grace by pulling into the parking lot of the Oak Tree Inn.

"Jake..."

"Happiness," he repeated. "You're a big girl, Gracie, and it's about time we all start treating you like one. I have a feeling I could learn something from Wiley Fortune in that regard. It's not up to me to determine what makes you happy. That's your decision. Now you just have to be brave enough to make it."

Her breath was coming out in shallow puffs. "What are you doing, Jake?"

After pulling to a stop in front of the inn, he reached over and opened the passenger-side door. "Hopefully giving you a little nudge in the right direction."

Too shocked to argue, Grace stepped out of the car. She'd barely closed the door when Jake took off, leaving her standing in the middle of nowhere in a cloud of dust.

"That wasn't exactly how he and I planned it."

She whirled around to the inn's front door to see Wiley walking toward her.

"You planned this?" Her brain felt like it was full of cotton, and her knees had gone weak. The thought that she could actually use her scooter or the crutches to help her balance almost made her smile. Almost.

"Jake agreed to bring you out here," Wiley said, his tone tentative. "I thought he was going to stay until we had a chance to talk."

"What if I don't want to talk?" she demanded, because it irritated her how good it felt to see him. She didn't want it to feel good. She wanted to stay strong and focused on the grand opening. That was her plan.

Wiley reached into the pocket of his dark jeans and pulled out a set of keys. "Take my car."

She narrowed her eyes. "So you had my brother drop me here, but you don't expect me to stay? I get that I'm tired, but I really don't understand what's going on right now."

"I should have asked Nicole or Megan for help," Wiley muttered, running an agitated hand through his hair. "They would have come up with a better plan. I'm sorry, Grace. I wanted tonight to be perfect. I thought if we were at a place that held good memories…" He gestured to the inn. "That first night we had dinner was one of the best nights of my life."

"Me, too," she whispered, suddenly nostalgic for the night when things had seemed so simple. He took a step forward, then stopped again.

"I asked your brother to help me win you back."

Grace choked back a snort. "And he agreed?"

Wiley shrugged. "He brought you to me, right?"

"I suppose he did." She glanced behind her, half expecting to see Jake come tearing back into the parking lot. "Wait." She turned back to Wiley. "You want to win me back?"

"More than anything," he confessed. "The fact is I'm miserable without you. It's like you brought the color to my life and now I'm stuck with boring black and white. I miss the color, Grace. I miss you."

She swallowed as emotion welled up in her throat. "It felt like you walked away without looking back," she told him. "You left for Chicago. You left me behind like I was nothing."

"I'm sorry." He moved closer until she could look up into his handsome face and see the golden flecks in his eyes. Heat radiated from him, and she had to force herself not to reach for him. She needed to stay strong. "I thought about you all the time. I hated being away from you."

"Why didn't you call?"

"I'm an idiot," he said with a harsh laugh. "I felt guilty that things had gone to hell back in Chicago while I was here with you. I told myself that I needed to make it right for the firm before I left the city. I thought you knew how I felt, Grace."

She shook her head.

"I love you," he whispered. "I think I fell a little bit in love that first night. Then I almost lost you before we ever had a chance."

Hope unfurled in her chest like a flower after a rainstorm. "What do you mean left the city?" As much as Grace loved hearing those three words from him, she was having trouble following this conversation. Did Wiley really—

"I quit my job," he said. "I'm going to join a firm out of Austin. Most of the work I do will be from Rambling Rose. I want to be here with you...for you."

He held up a hand when she would have spoken, and thank heaven for that because she had no idea how to respond. "But I'm staying no matter what you decide, Grace. I love you. That won't change. But even more, I respect you. I respect your strength and your integrity and the way you never give up. I don't want to give up on us, but the choice is yours."

Hers. He was giving her the power to decide her own fate, although Grace now realized she'd had it all along. She'd just been too scared to truly claim the life she wanted. Wiley had helped her see that she deserved to do just that.

Unable to resist one more moment, she threw her arms around him and pressed her mouth to his. "I love you, Wiley," she said against his lips. "I love the man you are and the way you believe in me. I love how you make me feel like I can do anything."

"You can, sweetheart." His arms tightened around her, and she could feel his heart thumping in his chest. "You can do anything, and I'm so damn grateful that you're choosing me. I will love you for always, Grace. I'm going to spend the rest of our lives proving that I'm the man who deserves you."

"You don't have to prove anything to me." She nuzzled her face into the crook of his neck, feeling like she'd finally come home. "I love you just the way you are."

He claimed her mouth again, kissing her until they were both breathless.

"Would you like to go upstairs?" he asked as he pulled away with a sexy grin.

"Did you get us a room here?" She grinned.

"I rented out the entire inn," he told her with a wink. "The whole place is ours for the night."

"And you're mine forever," she said. Joy exploded through her entire body, and she kissed him again.

* * * * *

Look for the next book in the new
Harlequin Special Edition continuity
The Fortunes of Texas: The Hotel Fortune

Their Second-Time Valentine
by Helen Lacey

On sale February 2021 wherever
Harlequin books and ebooks are sold.

#2815 WYOMING CINDERELLA

Dawson Family Ranch • by Melissa Senate

Molly Orton has loved Zeke Dawson since middle school. And now the scrappy single mom is ready to make her move. Except Zeke wants Molly to set him up with her knockout best friend! Molly knows if Zeke spends more time with her and her adorable baby, he'll see what love *really* looks like. All this plain Jane needs is a little Cinderella magic...

#2816 THEIR SECOND-TIME VALENTINE

The Fortunes of Texas: The Hotel Fortune • by Helen Lacey

Kane Fortune has never had any trouble attracting women—he's just never been the type to stick around. Until he meets widowed mom Layla McCarthy and her adorable toddler. But Layla's worried he's not up to the job of *lifetime* valentine. Kane will have his work cut out for him proving he's right for the role.

#2817 THE HOME THEY BUILT

Blackberry Bay • by Shannon Stacey

Host Anna Beckett knows clear well the Weaver house has never been a functioning inn, but taking the project got her to Blackberry Bay...the only place she'll ever find answers about her own family. Will her secrets threaten the budding romance between her and fake handyman Finn Weaver?

#2818 THE COWGIRL'S SURPRISE MATCH

Tillbridge Stables • by Nina Crespo

To keep the secret wedding plans from leaking to the press, Zurie Tillbridge and Mace Calderone must pretend *they* are the ones getting married. Cake tasting and flower arranging seem like harmless fun...until wary workaholic Zurie realizes she's feeling something real for her fake fiancé...

#2819 A SECRET BETWEEN US

Rancho Esperanza • by Judy Duarte

Pregnant waitress Callie Jamison was settling in to her new life in Fairborn, Montana, dividing her time between the ranch and the diner...and Ramon Cruz, the sexy town councilman, who never fails to show up for the breakfast shift. But will he still feel the same when he learns the secret Callie has been keeping?

#2820 HER MOUNTAINSIDE HAVEN

Gallant Lake Stories • by Jo McNally

Jillie Coleman has created a carefully constructed world for herself, complete with therapy dog Sophie, top-of-the-line security systems and a no-neighbors policy at her mountaintop retreat. But when intriguing developer Matt Danzer shows up, planning to develop the abandoned ski resort on the other side of the mountain, Jillie finds her stand-alone resolve starting to crumble...

SPECIAL EXCERPT FROM

ⓗ HARLEQUIN
SPECIAL EDITION

*Jillie's a bestselling horror writer who wants to be left
alone in her isolated mountainside cabin. Matt bought
the abandoned ski resort next door and plans to reopen
it. These uneasy neighbors battle over everything...*

Read on for a sneak peek at
Her Mountainside Haven,
*the next book in the Gallant Lake Stories
by Jo McNally.*

"And your secluded mountainside home with the
fancy electronics is part of that safety net? And your
hellhound?"

Jillie chuckled, looking up to where Sophie was
glaring down at Matt from the deck. "Don't insult my
dog. She's more for companionship than protection.
Although her appearance doesn't hurt." She shuddered
and pulled her jacket tighter.

God, he'd kept her standing out here in the cold and
dark while he grilled her with questions. She'd already
hinted that it was time for him to go. He scrubbed his
hands down his face.

"I'm sorry, Jillie. You must be freezing. Go on up.
Once I know you're inside, I'll take off."

"And you were on your way to dinner. You must
be starving." She hesitated for just a moment. In that
moment, he *really* wanted her to invite him up to join

her for dinner, but that didn't happen. Instead, she flashed him a quick smile before turning to go. "Thanks again, Matt."

Let her walk away. Way too complicated. Just let her walk away.

She was all the way up to the deck when he heard his own voice calling out to her.

"The old ski lift is working well, but I need to give it a few test runs, just to get acquainted with the thing. If you want a ride up to that craggy summit you like so much, I'll be heading up there Sunday afternoon. It'll just be us. No workers. No spectators."

Her head started to move back and forth, then stopped. She looked down at him in silence, then gave a loud sigh. "Maybe. I'll let you know. I've...I've got to go in."

He watched her and Sophie go through the door. She turned and locked it, then gave him a stuttering wave. For someone obsessed with privacy, it was interesting that this entire wall, right up to the peak of the A-frame roof, was glass. He lifted his hand, then headed to his car. He wasn't sure what surprised him more. That he'd asked Jillie to ride to the top of the mountain with him, or that she'd said maybe. As he turned the ignition, he realized he was smiling.

Don't miss
Her Mountainside Haven *by Jo McNally,*
available February 2021 wherever
Harlequin Special Edition books and ebooks are sold.

Harlequin.com

HSEEXP0121

Get 4 FREE REWARDS!

We'll send you 2 FREE Books plus 2 FREE Mystery Gifts.

Harlequin Special Edition books relate to finding comfort and strength in the support of loved ones and enjoying the journey no matter what life throws your way.

FREE Value Over $20